"You've been away long enough."

Marco glanced briefly at Sandra, then filled his glass with champagne. "Now you've come back you're going to stay. I want you here with me."

"Oh, really Marco," Sandra said with a nervous laugh. "How can you make me stay if I don't want to? When I left Venice last April I was leaving you for good. I'd found out you're a cheat, and I didn't want to live with you anymore."

"I know why you left," he retorted. "You'd been shaken out of that romantic dream in which I starred as a rich prince who had chosen you to be his bride to love happily ever after. You left because you found out suddenly that I'm human after all."

FLORA KIDD had a romantic dream—to own a sailboat and learn how to sail it. That dream came true when she found romance of another sort with a man who shared her love of the sea and became her husband and father of their four children. A native of Scotland, this bestselling romance author now lives in New Brunswick, one of Canada's maritime provinces, with the sea on her doorstep.

Books by Flora Kidd

Don't miss any of our special offers. Write to us at the following address for information on our newest releases.

Harlequin Reader Service
901 Fuhrmann Blvd., P.O. Box 1397, Buffalo, NY 14240
Canadian address: P.O. Box 603,
Fort Erie, Ont. L2A 5X3

FLORA KIDD

the married lovers

Harlequin Books

TORONTO • NEW YORK • LONDON
AMSTERDAM • PARIS • SYDNEY • HAMBURG
STOCKHOLM • ATHENS • TOKYO • MILAN

Harlequin Presents first edition July 1987
ISBN 0-373-10995-4

Original hardcover edition published in 1986
by Mills & Boon Limited

CHAPTER ONE

SANDRA was in the bathroom of the flat she shared with her friend, Thea, when she heard the phone ring. The bathroom door was pushed open and Thea appeared, her thin, monkeyish face alight with curiosity beneath her mop of brown curly hair.

'For you. Long distance. Person to person. From Italy, I think.'

Sandra nodded, finished rinsing her teeth, then followed Thea into the living-room. Sitting in the armchair placed near to the phone table, she picked up the receiver.

'Hello, Sandra Clarke here,' she said and heard the Italian operator instruct whoever was phoning to go ahead.

'Hello, Sandra.'

On hearing the deep voice she stiffened all over. It belonged to her husband, Marco Morosini, whom she hadn't seen for more than six months, not since she had run away from his apartment in Venice the previous April. The sound of his voice made her shiver uncontrollably with sense-inflaming excitement. Her lips tightened immediately and she gripped the receiver hard. She was tempted to bang it down on its rest, to hang up so that she wouldn't have to listen to him, wouldn't have to risk hearing his voice soften persuasively, seducing her with rich warm tones. But before she could move he spoke again, not softly, surprising her with a sharp note of authority. 'Sandra, are you still there?' he said.

'Yes, yes. I'm here.' Her voice was weaker than she would have liked it to be. Sitting up straight, she pushed back the deep wave of chestnut-coloured hair from her forehead, stiffened her chin and added in a harder voice, 'What do you want?'

There was a short pause. The line was very clear and she thought she could hear him breathing. Then he laughed, a brief, mocking sound.

'If I told you, you'd probably hang up,' he said; this time his voice did soften suggestively and she caught her breath sharply as she picked up the implication.

'Marco, be serious,' she warned him.

'I am serious. Claire has been hurt in a car accident,' he went on quickly, his voice crisp again. 'She's been asking for you. Now, listen carefully. I've booked a seat on a plane that leaves Heathrow tomorrow morning and flies directly to Venice. The time of departure is ten-fifty-five and it arrives here at fifteen-forty-five. You can pick up the ticket at the British Airways desk. Be on it, please, and I'll meet you and take you to see Claire.'

He was going too fast for her, as usual, stampeding her into agreeing to do what he suggested while she was still struggling to deal with the shock his blunt announcement of Claire's accident had given her.

'Wait. Stop,' she cried out. 'Oh, where is she?'

'In a hospital.'

'What injuries does she have?'

'I'm not sure,' He paused, then added in a lower voice that was roughened by some emotion, 'You must come, Sandra. You must come to see her.'

'When did the accident happen?'

'Two days ago.'

'Two days ago?' she exclaimed. 'Then why didn't you let me know at once?'

'I didn't know about it until this afternoon. I've been trying to get in touch with you all evening. I'll meet you tomorrow.' He was coldly autocratic again, the clear-sighted, highly-organised businessman issuing orders.

'But I'm not sure I can catch that plane. I'll have to ask for time off from the library ...'

'You'll come tomorrow, Sandra, or you'll be sorry,' he threatened harshly. 'I must go now. *Arrivederci*.'

He hung up before she could think of any more arguments, and she returned the receiver to its rest. Sitting there alone, she could hear her heart beating fast, feel the blood boiling in her veins. Oh, damn Marco, damn him! She clutched her face between her hands as she tried to control the shudders of reaction that were shaking through her. Why was it that just the sound of his voice could do this to her? For the last few months, ever since she had left him, she had managed to avoid speaking to him even though he had phoned her, having got hold of the number of Thea's apartment somehow, probably from Joan. She had also ignored the two letters he had written to her and, when he had made a trip to London on business, knowing he would be coming, she had fled from the city and had hidden for those few days.

Why? Because she was afraid of him; afraid of what he could do to her; afraid he might take over her life again.

The door to the kitchenette opened and Thea came into the living-room. She was holding a mug from which steam was rising.

'Like some Ovaltine?' she asked in her casual yet kindly way. 'You look a bit pale. I hope it wasn't bad news.'

'My mother has been hurt in a car crash in Italy.

She's asking for me; I'll have to go to her tomorrow. A seat has been booked for me on a flight to Venice,' replied Sandra dully. She took the steaming mug from Thea. 'Thanks,' she said with a wan smile.

Thea curled up in a corner of the settee and studied Sandra thoughtfully. The lemon-coloured, quilted dressing-gown Sandra was wearing enhanced the rich sheen of her tawny hair which was cut in a short, smooth bob following the natural curve of its deep waves. Thea thought her friend, although pale, looked as composed as usual, until she noticed how frantically a pulse was beating in Sandra's white throat and how she was picking at a thread in the dressing-gown with a finger and thumb. Any expression in Sandra's eyes was hidden by the downward sweep of long, dark lashes that Thea had always envied.

'Now, let me get this straight,' Thea said. 'You said your mother has been in an accident in Italy. The mother you're referring to is your natural mother, your *real* mother, I take it, the mother you went to see and to stay with in Venice about eighteen months ago? You're not talking about Joan Clarke, your adoptive mother?'

'No. I'm not talking about Joan,' replied Sandra after sipping some of the Ovaltine.

'And that was him, wasn't it? Your husband, Marco?' persisted Thea curiously. 'He's phoned before; I recognised his voice, deep and enigmatic. What did he say about your mother?'

'He said Claire has been asking for me. He said that if I don't go tomorrow to see her I'll be sorry.' Sandra paused to control her voice which had begun to rise shakily. 'Oh, Thea,' she whispered, 'do you think he means she might die?'

'I really can't say,' replied Thea practically, her

hazel eyes compassionate, 'not knowing much about her injuries.' Her eyes narrowed shrewdly. 'Did he tell you how badly she's injured?'

'No. He said he didn't know.'

'Do you think he's telling the truth?' asked Thea. Her experience with the opposite sex had not given her a very good opinion of men. She was inclined to believe they were all liars.

Sandra looked up, her grey, green-flecked eyes widening. For all her twenty-five years she looked very young, thought Thea wryly; young and innocent, easily fooled.

'Why would he lie about an accident?' Sandra exclaimed.

'To get you to fly out to Venice; to get you in his power again!' said Thea dramatically. Then, with a little laugh at her own histrionics, she said more normally, 'Perhaps he's pining for you and wants you back.'

'I can't imagine Marco pining for any woman,' sighed Sandra, visualising her handsome self-confident husband and remembering how many times she had seen other women making up to him. 'He wouldn't have to,' she added rather drearily. 'He'd just have to snap his fingers and any woman he wanted would come running.'

'Any woman except you, you mean,' murmured Thea. 'Are you still in love with him?'

The question disconcerted Sandra because she didn't know the right answer. For weeks, for months, she had been trying to find the answer to it and had failed.

'I don't know,' she muttered. 'There are times when I think I hate him because . . . oh, because of what he can do to me.' She glanced appealingly at Thea as if her friend might be able to help her find the answer to the question. 'How can I love him when I know he doesn't love me? It takes two to love and build a secure and fulfilling relationship. You know that as well as I do.'

'True enough, I do,' replied Thea with a wry twist of her lips. 'But what has Marco done to make you think he doesn't love you?'

'He married me because he knew I was Claire's daughter,' said Sandra cryptically.

'So?' Thea prompted, raising her eyebrows. 'What has being Claire's daughter got to do with it?'

'It's all very complicated. You see, Claire inherited more than half the shares in the Fontelli company when Francesco died.'

'Are you trying to tell me that Marco married you because he believed you might one day inherit Claire's shares in the company?' exclaimed Thea, her voice lilting with incredulity. 'That had to be very far-sighted of him, very cool and calculating.'

'I know. But you see, he's like that,' Sandra said, recalling the angry scene with Marco when she had accused him of marrying her not for love but because it would be advantageous to him to be married to the daughter of the Fontelli company's chairperson. 'And he didn't deny it,' she added. 'But there was another reason. There was Lucia.'

'Who's she?' asked Thea.

'His mistress.' Sandra almost spat the word out.

'Aha. Now we're getting to the nub of the matter,' drawled Thea knowingly, her eyes beginning to twinkle with mockery again. 'Lucia, the other woman. She sounds more like a good reason for leaving him than the other. I'd have left too if I'd found out he was

cheating on me.' She paused and frowned thoughtfully. 'But if he's a deceiver he could be lying about your
mother's accident, couldn't he?'

'I suppose he could,' murmured Sandra miserably.
'Oh, I don't know what to do. I don't know how I can
find out if she's in hospital or not. Or where.'

'Supposing she *is* hurt and asking for you, would you
really want to go to her?' asked Thea probingly.

'Oh, yes,' Sandra answered without hesitation. 'I
wasn't with Claire for very long, but during that time I
learned to love her.'

'Even though you knew she had deserted you when
you were only six months old?'

'She didn't really desert me. She left me with Joan
and Ed, and no one could have had a better home than
I had with them. They couldn't have done more for me
if I'd been their own child. I have to thank them for a
happy childhood and the opportunity of a good
education. I wouldn't have had that if Claire had tried
to struggle on as a single parent.'

'Why did she leave you with the Clarkes? Do you
know? Has she ever told you?'

'Yes, she has. Both she and Joan have told me and
their stories tally,' said Sandra. 'You see, Claire met
Count Francesco Fontelli, a wealthy Venetian . . .'

'Where? Where did she meet him?' Thea interrupted.

'Here. In London. He was here on business and he
went to see a play in which Claire had a small part. He
was attracted to her and went backstage to meet her.
He asked her to marry him on one condition. He said
he didn't want to be a stepfather to me and if she
agreed to marry him she would have to give me up,
find a decent home for me to live in.'

'My God, how selfish can a man get,' exclaimed

Thea. 'Had he been married before? Did he have children?'

'Not as far as I know. He was older than Claire, about twenty years older, so he was about forty-five when they met. Claire was tired of trying to make her living as an actress and she saw that as his wife she wouldn't only have comfort and luxury but she would be able to provide a good home for me with the money he allowed her.'

'I can't understand how you can love her if she is so selfish too,' argued Thea. 'She put herself first and left you, abandoned you.'

'No, she didn't,' retorted Sandra, her quick temper rising as she defended Claire. 'If she had abandoned me she wouldn't have gone to so much trouble to find a good home for me. She would have just put me in an orphanage or somewhere like that. Joan Clarke and she had been friends for years, since childhood. So she went to Joan with her dilemma and Joan and Ed offered to adopt me. They had one daughter already, Laura, but had found out Joan couldn't have any more babies so they were delighted to take me in.' Sandra broke off to calm herself, and went on in a quieter voice. 'You'd have to meet and know Claire to love her. She may put herself first, but she's never harmed anyone else by doing so, and she did what she did for me because she felt it was the best for me. And it was.'

'All right, all right,' Thea said soothingly. 'I get the message. But what made you want to know who your real mother was? I suppose Joan never told you about Claire, as is usual in cases of adoption?'

'She told me I was adopted, but she never told me the name of my mother or my father. I read an article in a newspaper about two years ago concerning a woman who had found her natural mother years after her adoption so I asked Joan if she would tell me about my real mother. She did, and she said she didn't think Claire would mind if I wrote to her. So I wrote and Claire wrote back telling me that Francesco Fontelli had just died and inviting me to go and stay with her so we could get to know each other.' Sandra broke off to bite her lip. 'Now I wish I hadn't agreed to stay longer with her and had come back to England as I'd planned after spending my two weeks' holiday with her,' she muttered.

'Why do you wish that?'

'Isn't it obvious? If I hadn't stayed on I wouldn't have married Marco, and chances are he and I would never have seen each other again.'

'Well, it's no good crying over spilt milk now,' said Thea practically. 'What's done is done; it's how to undo it that's the problem. What exactly does he have to do with Fontelli's?'

'What do you know about Fontelli's?'

'I know they have shops all over the world. And I've been in their shop here, in London. Beautiful glassware, silverware, pottery and china. The best handcrafted stuff from most countries, they seem to stock. It must be quite an organisation to have access to all those small industries that produce elegantly designed handmade ornaments and to market them all over the world.'

'It is quite an organisation, and it was started by Francesco Fontelli when he inherited a glassware factory in Venice. He decided to expand the business, make it more than just a factory producing and selling Venetian glass for tourists to buy. He had a very good eye for the best in design, and he insisted that the glassware made in his factory should be of the best quality; he would sell it abroad in shops that he controlled. That turned out to be successful, and he found that there was a demand for well-designed handmade things. So he went around looking for small cottage industries producing handmade goods in every country in Europe, sometimes taking them over, sometimes making them associates of Fontelli so that he could command the supply of elegant wares to his shops. There is one industry in Scotland that comes under the Fontelli umbrella.'

'Morison's silver and pewter!' exclaimed Thea. 'How I'd love to own one of their silver mugs. But they're really pricey.'

'Everything that is sold at Fontelli's is expensive, but everything is of the best design, contemporary as well as traditional. The company is a great patron of contemporary craftsmen and artists.'

'So what does Marco do in this empire called Fontelli's?' Thea asked.

'He's now the financial controller. I think that one day he'll be the managing director. He's a very shrewd businessman, and full of ideas for marketing and acquiring new small industries.'

'A whizz-kid, eh?' remarked Thea. 'He can't be all that old.'

'He's just nine years older than I am.'

'And accustomed to getting his own way, I bet,' remarked Thea drily. 'Another selfish blighter wanting his cake and eating it too. He'd have done better to have married a placid, forgiving type of woman rather than an independent spitfire like you if he wanted to keep a mistress on the side.'

'That's what I think, too,' said Sandra miserably. 'And that's why I have to believe he married me because he knew I was Claire's daughter and she owns the controlling shares in the company.'

'Mmm. I see your point,' drawled Thea, her eyes narrowing thoughtfully. 'But have you ever thought, Sandra, you've got him over a barrel if there is any truth in this other woman affair. You could file for divorce and get a big settlement out of him.'

'No, I've never thought of that,' said Sandra sharply. 'And I won't. Thea, would you do me a favour? Would you drive me to Heathrow in the morning to catch that plane?'

'If you're really sure it's what you want to do. Shouldn't you check on the story of your mother's accident first?'

'I don't see how I can?'

'What about your mother's servants in Venice? Couldn't you call her number and find out if they know anything about her?'

'I suppose I could call Luigi. He looks after the apartment for her,' said Sandra reluctantly. 'But it's late, nearly midnight. He'll be in bed.' She was beginning to realise that she wanted to go to Venice to see Claire; she wanted to obey Marco's summons. She didn't want to find out that he had been lying.

'Then call him early in the morning,' suggested Thea, stifling a yawn with her hand. She uncurled herself and stood up. 'I'm going to bed,' she said. Just then the phone rang again. Sandra picked up the receiver.

'Sandra Clarke here,' she said, nerving herself against hearing Marco's voice again.

'Sandy. I had to phone,' said Joan Clarke rather breathlessly. 'I know it's late but since you haven't phoned me I just wondered if Marco managed to reach you. He phoned me about nine o'clock. He's been trying to get hold of you. He had bad news about Claire, I'm afraid.'

'Yes, yes. I know. He phoned here again and I was in. I'd been out to the concert at the Festival Hall with Kevin Collins. He told me about Claire, said she was asking for me.'

'You're going, aren't you? He said he'd made arrangements for you to fly out tomorrow. You must go, Sandy.' Joan spoke with motherly authority. 'You must go to see her. And let me know as soon as you have. Phone me immediately. I do hope she isn't badly hurt.'

'I hope she isn't too. Did . . . did Marco say anything to you about her injuries?'

'He just said it was important for you to go, that you might be sorry if you didn't go,' replied Joan. 'And ever since I've been thinking the worst, that she might die.'

'I've been thinking that too,' whispered Sandra. 'I'm going, Mum.' She would never get out of the habit of calling Joan Mum.

'Is there anything you want me to do for you while you're away? Should I phone the library at the Institute and tell them you've had to go away?' offered Joan.

'No, thanks. I'll do that in the morning; there'll be time before the plane takes off. I'll phone John MacKendrick from the airport and ask for compassionate leave. Goodnight, Mum.'

She rang off and turned to Thea who had lingered in the doorway of the living-room, listening.

'Well?' Thea queried.

'Marco was telling the truth,' Sandra said, rising to her feet. 'He wouldn't have rung Joan if he had been trying to trick me into flying to Venice.'

'I suppose he wouldn't have,' murmured Thea, but she sounded unconvinced. 'I wish I still had your naïveté, your trust in human nature,' she added wryly. 'Or maybe I should say, your trust in the opposite sex.'

'Don't worry,' retorted Sandra. 'I'm not as naïve as I was when I first went to Venice a year and half ago, and I feel much older.'

'You are,' mocked Thea. 'But you don't look it.'

'I've been soured by the experience of marriage to Marco,' said Sandra with a wry grin.

'You don't look soured. But you're more reserved than you used to be. A little haunted-looking,' observed Thea shrewdly. 'More the angel who fears to tread than the fool who rushes in. Perhaps you're considering a divorce, at last. You should, you know.' Thea herself had been married and divorced. 'You could tell Marco when he meets you. Who knows, he might welcome the suggestion.'

'I'll think about it. Tomorrow, on the flight to Venice,' replied Sandra cautiously. 'What time should we leave for the airport?'

'I'll set my alarm for seven,' said Thea. 'I'd like to get you there early because I have to be in the office by ten. Important editorial meeting for the next edition of the magazine.' Thea was a graphic designer at a publishing company on the South Bank.

'I suppose I could go by tube,' murmured Sandra.

'No, I'll drive you, make sure you get there.'

Sandra didn't sleep at all that night for thinking about Claire and then about Marco, reliving many moments of her first visit to Venice.

She had set out so eagerly that April a year and a half ago, flying first to Milan and then going by train to Venice. She had been looking forward to meeting her natural mother with never a thought for the other people she might meet, never an inkling that her own impetuosity would lead her into the dark, tortuous, yet curiously flame-lit labyrinths of passionate love.

How well she could remember her arrival at the Stazione Santa Lucia after crossing the Ponte della Liberta which joins the island of Venice to the mainland. As she had followed the porter, who had been pushing her luggage in a small cart out of the terminus, she had felt damp air caress her face and she had smelled the sea. The Piazzale della Stazione had been all rush and bustle as tourists who had arrived on the train had swarmed across the square to the landing stages on the Grand Canal, and for a few moments of bewilderment she had wondered how the person whom Claire had said would meet her at the station would find her and recognise her.

'Marco will meet you,' Claire had said during the phone call she had made to the Clarkes' home before Sandra had left. 'You can depend on it. He will be there.'

On the other side of the canal, buildings of pinkish bricks with red-tiled roofs had glowed in the spring sunshine, and the green cupola of the church of San Simeon Piccola had glittered against a bright blue sky. Excited and fascinated by the sound of Italian voices all around her, and the narrow gleam of the water of the canal, Sandra hadn't noticed a man coming straight towards her until he stopped in front of her, blocking her way, and spoke to her.

She had stopped just short of bumping into him and had looked up into a lean suntanned face lit by two light grey eyes.

'Sandra Clarke?'

'Oh! How did you know I'm Sandra Clarke?' she

had exclaimed. 'How *did* you know?'

'I guessed,' he had replied coolly.

With a rush of embarrassment, she had realised she had spoken automatically to him in English and had tried to rectify her mistake in stumbling Italian. He had cut short her apology brusquely, speaking in clear unaccented English.

'I understand and speak English better than you do Italian,' he said coldly. 'I'm Marco Morosini. The Contessa Fontelli asked me to meet you. Come this way,'

Overwhelmed by his dark good looks and the arrogance with which he had taken charge of her, whisking her and her luggage from the station exit through the crowds of people to the landing place, Sandra had let him help her aboard a sleek varnished speedboat with a small cabin. In a few seconds they had left the landing stage behind, surging out into the canal, dodging at speed among *vaporetti* and gondolas.

She had seen hardly anything on that first trip along the canal, had been only vaguely aware of the Rialto Bridge looming up, before the speedboat had passed under it, and of the ancient and stately palaces and churches that had seemed to grow out of the water. She had been too interested in Marco. She had sat in the cockpit of the speedboat and stared and stared at him.

Never in all her life, until that point in time, had she come in contact with anyone like him. A person of contrasts, with jet-black hair and light grey eyes, his severely chiselled features cold and unsmiling, hinting at an inner discipline that was at variance with the reckless yet competent way he had steered the boat through the afternoon water-traffic, he had drawn her attention to him like a magnet. Younger-looking than

his years, square-shouldered and lean-hipped, he had
been dressed with the casual elegance she would
always associate with him, in well-fitting designer
jeans, a crisp white shirt, open at the neck, and a bulky
Italian sweater with a dropped shoulder line and wide
armholes patterned in red and black.

He had guided the boat down a side canal stopping
it at the back of an old restored building between two
striped mooring poles, the stripes painted in the
colours of the Fontelli family. Up some steps, through
a double door and into a quiet passageway he had led
her, round to the front entrance where they had
entered a lift and, although she had been bursting with
questions, she hadn't spoken, intimidated more than a
little by his silence and his aloof attitude. Not until he
had delivered her to Claire's penthouse apartment at
the top of the restored Fontelli palace and had left, had
she spoken, her curiosity about him bursting out.

'Who is he?' she had demanded and, looking back
now, she realised she had been far more interested in
Marco than she had in meeting Claire.

'Marco? Oh, he's with the company, director in
charge of finance—a real wizard when it comes to
predicting the company's future. You could say he's
Francesco's natural successor, and I wouldn't be at all
surprised if he didn't take over the management
completely, one day,' Claire had replied casually.
'He's been marvellous to me, I couldn't have managed
the chairmanship without his help.'

Claire had been so different from Joan. Poised and
chic, her silvery blonde hair beautifully coiffured in
small waves, she had been wearing a model dress of
black silk that day. She had fitted into the décor of the
luxuriously appointed apartment as if it had been
designed around her, and she told Sandra that when

he had married her, Francesco had had the whole place re-decorated and renovated.

It had taken Sandra some time to adjust to living in such luxury and to living with a woman who called her darling all the time. But she had liked Claire from the moment of meeting her. There had been no traumatic scenes, no tears, no bitterness. Claire had welcomed her as if she had been a favourite niece and Sandra had welcomed the role, although she had been a little surprised when Claire had said, 'I don't want to tell anyone you're my daughter while you're here.'

'But why not?'

'For various reasons, one being that I have never mentioned you to any of Francesco's relatives or friends because he asked me not to. He said it was none of their business.'

'Does that mean Marco doesn't know?' That had been Sandra's first concern.

'Yes. He just thinks you're the daughter of an old schoolfriend of mine, which is true in a way because you're much more Joan's daughter than you are mine.' Her blue glance had swept over Sandra's clothing. 'A daughter I'd brought up wouldn't be seen dead in an outfit like that, for a start,' she had remarked scornfully. 'Another reason I dont want anyone to know you're my daughter is quite a silly one. I don't want anyone to know I'm older that I look. If I introduce you as my daughter they'll take one look at you and start guessing I'm over forty.'

'Well, aren't you?'

'A few years only, but I'm not going to tell you how many,' Claire had retorted. 'It's a good thing you look more like Charlton than me.'

'Who's Charlton?'

'Your father, darling. He had red hair and green eyes, too.'

'My hair isn't red, it's chestnut-brown, and my eyes aren't green. They're greenish grey,' Sandra had retorted huffily, and Claire had laughed delightedly.

'Oh dear, oh dear. Do you have a temper like Charlton's too?' she had scoffed. 'All right, then, I'll let you have it. Chestnut and greenish-grey. Most attractive.'

'Where is my father now?' Sandra had asked eagerly. 'Do you know? Do you keep in touch with him?'

'To do that I'd have to be one of those weird people who communicates with the dead, darling,' Claire had replied and had continued sadly, 'I'm afraid Charlie died, my dear, soon after you were born. He was in the theatre too.'

'An actor?'

'One of the best younger actors in English repertory at the time.' Claire had sighed and then had smiled sweetly. 'He was ten years older than I, and he smoked too much. He died of lung cancer.'

It had been then that Sandra had asked a question that had often bothered her and to which Joan had never been able to supply an answer.

'Could you . . . would you tell me, please, if you and he were married to each other?'

'Yes. We were. After you were born. You were six years old at the time. Charlie was determined your birth should be legitimised. He died a year later. Is that a load off your mind, darling?' Claire had been gentle and understanding.

'Yes. Thank you for telling me.'

'You're welcome,' Claire had replied absently, staring off into space as she relived some moments of her past. 'When he saw you lying in my arms with your golden hair and pale skin he wanted so desperately to live to see you grow up. But it was too late. His bad habits and wild way of life caught up on him.' There had been a sad little silence as they had both mourned Charlton, and then Claire had given herself a little shake and said, 'Well, it's no use looking backwards all the time. Never have regrets, that's what Charlie always said. Always look forward and be positive. We'll really have to do something about how you look while you're staying with me. I'd like you to be smarter. That skirt you're wearing is badly seated, and the blouse is so plain! Oh, it's going to be such fun taking you around and getting you fitted out with some new clothes.'

'But I can't afford many clothes,' Sandra had protested.

'But I can,' Claire had replied with an air of triumph. 'I'm wealthy, darling. Francesco not only left me an allowance for life but he also left me half the shares in the Fontelli company and nominated me his successor as chairman. I can spend as much as I like on you. Oh, I'm so glad you've come to me. You're just what I need to lift me out of the doldrums of boredom.'

It had been fun being fitted out with clothes she had never hoped to own, and it was during those shopping sprees in the many fashion boutiques of Venice that she had learned to know and love Claire.

But it had been Marco who had shown her the real Venice. One day when she had been leaving the Fontelli *palazzo*, intending to go for a walk, she had chanced to meet him in the entrance hall as he was returning, she had guessed at the time, from Mestre where the head offices of Fontelli Enterprises were located. When she had seen him, remote and handsome in a lightweigt business suit striding past her without noticing her, she had almost flung herself in his path so that she had literally bumped into him.

'Oh, it's you,' she had exclaimed, hoping that her acting was up to the standard of Claire's.

His light eyes had regarded her coldly for several unnerving moments and she had wondered if he had forgotten all about her.

'Sandra Clarke,' she had said breathlessly. 'I . . . I'm staying with the Contessa Fontelli.'

'I remember,' he had murmured, and she had wondered then if he had been telling the truth or just being polite. 'How are you?' he had asked. 'Enjoying your stay? You must have been here nearly two weeks now.'

'Ten days, I'll be going back to England on Saturday of this week.'

'So soon?' He had frowned. 'Why do you have to go back?'

'To work. I have to work for my living,' she had replied with a little laugh.

'But I would have thought . . .' he had begun, broken off, frowned some more, then shrugged. 'No matter,' he had gone on and had smiled suddenly, a smile that made his eyes glow warmly and his even white teeth flash in his lean sun-bronzed face; a smile that had lit up her whole life and had enticed her to fall in love with him on the spot. 'I hope you have enjoyed Venice,' he said.

'I've tried to but Claire doesn't like sightseeing and so I've had to look around on my own,' she had replied. 'And that isn't much fun. I need to have someone with me to share my delight in places, if you know what I mean.'

'I know what you mean,' he had said softly, and

although he hadn't smiled the warmth had still been in his eyes as he had looked at her intently. 'Have you been for a ride in a gondola yet?'

'No. They're quite expensive . . .' she had begun to explain when he had cut in arrogantly,

'We'll go now. Come on.'

And to her secret amazement he had taken hold of her arm and urged her out of the front door of the palace and along the quay of San Marco to the place where the gondolas were moored.

From that day onwards her life had changed dramatically as Marco had taken over the direction of it. Instead of returning to England and the public library in Surrey, she had stayed on in Venice, invited by Claire to stay all summer if she wanted. Lately she had begun to wonder if Marco had been behind that invitation, if, after having discovered she was Claire's daughter, he had persuaded her mother to invite her to stay longer so that he would have time to court her, seduce her and marry her.

But she hadn't thought that at the time. In love for the first time in her life, she had stayed on, willingly resigning from her job in England because she had wanted to be with or near Marco.

How wonderful that summer had been when he had introduced her to the delights of Venice, sharing with her his own deep knowledge of the city's history and its art treasures, taking her to the Lido in his speedboat to swim and sunbathe on the shores of the Adriatic, and sometimes driving her into the dramatic and craggy scenery of the Dolomites to a chalet he rented there, near Cortina, and from which, in the winter, he ski'd the steep slopes.

It was while staying at the chalet one weekend that they had become lovers and she had ceased to be an innocent schoolgirl and had blossomed into a woman of deep and passionate emotions. When Marco had asked her marry him she had no hesitation in agreeing. They had been married quietly and secretly during another weekend visit to the mountains.

Claire hadn't been at all surprised when Sandra had broken the news to her.

'Anyone with perception could see it coming,' she had teased lightly.

'You don't mind, then, about the way we've done it?' Sandra had queried anxiously. She had been worried incase Claire might object to the secrecy of the wedding.

'Not at all. It's your life, after all, and I know darned well I wouldn't have liked any interference from my parents when I was your age,' Claire had replied. She had given Sandra a sharp glance. 'You haven't told him you're my daughter, have you?'

'No, but I'd like to. I feel everything ought to be straight and open between us,' Sandra had said earnestly. 'I feel we should know all there is to know about each other and . . .'

'No,' Claire had interrupted, looking almost stern. 'Never make that mistake. Never tell a man every-thing about yourself. Leave something for him to find out on his own. You can be sure Marco hasn't told you everything about himself. I bet you don't know who hisparents are or were, or where he comes from, do you?'

'No, I don't,' Sandra had admitted.

'Neither does anyone else. Except Francesco, of course, and he won't tell. Not now,' Claire had laughed a little and then had hugged Sandra with affection. 'I do hope you'll be happy,' she had whispered. 'I hope nothing happens to spoil it for you.'

* * *

Sandra groaned, turned over and peered at the digital alarm clock. The red numbers informed her that it was five-twenty-six. In another half-hour she could get up and make some coffee. It wasn't the first time she had had a sleepless night since she had left Marco last April. He was the sort of person you had sleepless nights about as you wondered all the time if you could have handled him differently, or if you should have been less committed in your love for him and behaved more independently from the start.

If only Lucia Spenola hadn't come to Venice on a visit last Spring. Lucia had some sort of connection with Fontelli's and had been the same age as Marco. Lean, dark and sharply witty, she had known him in the States. She had been friendly towards Sandra and had told her much about him. Too much. Lucia had told her Marco had known that Sandra was Claire's daughter long before he had married her.

'He knows you're Claire's daughter. Why else would he marry you?' Lucia had said scornfully. 'You ought to know by now that Marco doesn't have to marry a woman to get what he wants from her. Or did you hold out against him? Somehow I don't think so.'

'Then why do you think he married me?' Sandra had forced herself to ask.

'So that those shares Claire owns don't go out of the sphere of the Fontelli family. He's married you because one day you might inherit those shares from Claire. And also, perhaps, a little to be revenged on Claire. You see, Francesco left no shares to Marco, none at all, so Marco resents Claire, always has.' Lucia's smile had been bright and wicked. 'And he is half Italian, you know, and was brought up in Italy, and we Italians are a vengeful people.'

But, not content with having sown that seed of suspicion in Sandra's mind, Lucia also hinted that she and Marco had always been very close and that when he had been in the States recently he had renewed their affair, which had started when he had been studying in Philadelphia for a postgraduate degree.

The alarm clock began to ring, and she reached out to stop it. Thank God, it was time to get up. She had had enough of lying in the dark, remembering. Leaving the bed, she went from bedroom to kitchenette to put on the coffee-maker. Then she went to the bathroom to shower, hoping that stinging hot water would sluice away the feeling of dragging weariness.

Everything that morning went according to plan. Thea drove her to Heathrow and said goodbye with a warning.

'Don't let that husband of yours take you over again. Whatever you do, don't give in to him. I had this problem with Jack, you know, and I was well rid of him.'

'I'll try not to give in,' Sandra murmured. She had met Jack Driscoll, Thea's ex-husband, once only and could agree entirely that Thea was well rid of him. There was no comparison between him and Marco, and she wondered vaguely if, having been married to Marco instead, Thea would have wanted to be rid of *him*.

After getting the ticket that Marco had arranged to be waiting for her at the airline desk, she checked in her one suitcase and then went to phone the senior librarian at the Institute of Anthropology where she had been working on a part-time basis for the past few months. She told him she needed time off to visit her mother who was in hospital in Italy and promised to return to work the following Monday morning. Then she went through the security check and into the departure lounge to await the calling of the flight to Venice.

CHAPTER TWO

IT was surprising how her spirits lifted as soon as the plane began its descent to Venice airport, thought Sandra. Surprising, too, how the feeling of tiredness faded away. Why? Because she was nearly at her destination and would soon be seeing the domes and towers of the magical city glowing and flashing in the last rays of the sun? Or was it because she would soon be seeing Marco again?

She had collected her suitcase and was walking out of the terminal building when he walked up to her. He was wearing an expensive sheepskin jacket open over a light grey suit. His black hair was windblown and his face was pale, hollows in his cheeks accentuating his cheekbones. He looked as if he felt cold.

'How is Claire?' She forced the words out past a thickness in her throat, a choking-up she felt on seeing him again after being such a long time away from him.

His eyes glittered with a wintry light as he glanced down at her. He didn't show any sign of being pleased to see her.

'She's making progress,' he replied non-committally, and took her case from her. 'We go this way to the car.'

'I'd like to go to the hospital straight away to see her. I'll stay in a hotel nearby,' she said rather breathlessly as she hurried to keep up with him, determined to assert her independence from him and to state her plan of action. The wind was cold, and damp was now seeping through the thin tweed of her suit, and she wished she had worn her thick winter coat instead of a raincoat.

He didn't say anything, but strode among the parked cars until he reached his own car, the same Ferrari sports he had owned when she had left. He put her case in the back, opened the door on the passenger's side for her and walked round to the driver's side.

Sandra got in and was immediately reminded of all the other times she had ridden in that car. The smooth suede of the seat cover cushioned her. The elusive scent of the cigars Marco sometimes smoked tantalised her nose. Warmth from the heater caressed her legs and hands, which were chilly from the walk to the car, as Marco drove skilfully through the traffic.

Comfort, fast transport—she had possessed both while she had lived with him, and not only while she had lived with him. That day, she had flown first class on a ticket he had provided. He had given her everything any woman could want—expensive well-designed clothes, jewellery—and he had shared his luxurious apartment with her. Everything money could buy had been hers. So why had she left him?

She glanced sideways at him. Clearcut and severe, his profile was dark against the pale November sunlight outside. As at their first meeting Sandra was fascinated by the paradox he presented. Light northern eyes glistening frostily; jet-black hair and a southern olive-tinted complexion. Coldly remote one minute, warmly open the next. A disciplined, forceful businessman inhabiting the same skin as an extravagant, generous hedonist. The answer to her question as to why she had left him came to her in a flash. She had left him because he had never given himself to her entirely. He had always held something back, had never allowed her to know all of him and so she had never really been sure of him. She had never been sure he loved her.

She looked away from him and out of the windscreen. They were approaching the Ponte della Liberta and she could see the gold-tinted water of the lagoon flat as a sheet of shining silk. Beyond the shimmer of water the *campaniles* and roofs of Venice floated like a brilliant yet ghostly dream of beauty.

'This isn't the way to the hospital,' she said sharply.

'Which hospital?' He was cool, laconic.

'The hospital in Mestre.'

'Why would you want to go there?' As always he was indifferent to the irritation she was feeling that showed itself in the rising of her voice. He didn't even glance at her or slow down. The car surged on to the bridge, leaving behind the dark industrial buildings of Merghera and Mestre, satanic shapes looming over mudflats fouled with waste.

Trying to subdue an urge to shout and scream at him, to rant and rave at his indifference, Sandra gripped her hands together and bit hard on her lower lip. When she felt she could speak calmly she said, 'Which hospital is she in, then?'

'She was taken to hospital in Milan. The accident happened near there,' he replied, and the car sped on across the long causeway. On the flat lagoon a few small fishing boats lolled idly.

'Why didn't you tell me that last night when you phoned me? Why didn't you book a seat for me on a flight to Milan?' she exclaimed.

'Because I knew I would not be in Milan to meet you,' he said smoothly.

'That's a downright silly reason,' she protested.

'You didn't have to be there to meet me. I could have found my own way to the hospital if you'd told me which one she was in. I'm quite capable of looking after myself. I don't need you around all the time to meet me and drive me to places. Now, please will you take me back to the airport. I'll try and get on a flight to Milan this evening.'

'No.'

They were almost at the end of the causeway. She could see the outline of the modern station building next to the baroque dome of the Scalzi church. Then they were swerving to the right to approach the Piazzale Roma by way of San Chiara. She knew the names of more buildings in Venice, she realised, than she did of buildings in London, and it was all thanks to the man who sat beside her.

Marco parked the car in the busy Piazzale Roma, the terminus on the island for buses and cars. Staring at the coloured buses, Sandra wondered which one went to Milan. As soon as she stepped out of the car she went round to Marco who was taking her case out of the back. The sound of bus engines throbbing and the cries of seagulls were all around them and the wind was even colder and damper.

'I'll go to Milan by bus.' She raised her voice slightly to make sure he had heard her. 'Please give me my case.'

Without answering he locked the car doors, still carrying her case.

'Marco, I'm not coming with you,' she stated firmly. 'Give me my case and tell me which hospital in Milan Claire is in.'

'You can go to see her later. Maybe tomorrow or maybe the day after,' he replied with a shrug. 'We'll go to the apartment now.'

'I'm not coming with you and you can't make me go with you,' she retorted.

'You think not?' His black eyebrows lifted in scornful amusement and his lips slanted in a grin. 'I don't mind picking you up and carrying you on to a *vaporetto*. I'm sure it would provide entertainment for the other passengers.' He dropped her case to the ground and stepped forward, his arms reaching for her, his eyes glinting with amusement. 'Perhaps it is what you would really like me to do,' he suggested mockingly.

'No, I wouldn't.' She backed away from him. 'I don't understand. Why have you tricked me into coming here? Why couldn't you have arranged for me to fly to Milan?'

For answer he turned on his heel, picked up her case again, and strode off in the direction of the landing stage. After one more glance at the line of buses Sandra gave in and followed him with Thea's warning ringing in her ears. *Don't let that husband of yours take over. Don't give in to him.*

She had no choice, she argued with herself as she walked on to the waiting *vaporetto* after him. After all, he had her suitcase and he knew where Claire was. She sat inside the cabin far away from him. The waterbus was only half full, most of the passengers being tourists, accompanied by a tour guide, who were taking advantage of off-season rates and lack of crowds.

As the *vaporetto* chugged along the Grand Canal, Sandra stared out at the old buildings edging the water. Palaces and warehouses sat side by side, their stone façades glowing pink in the light of the setting sun. Watching them slide by, she thought how incredible it was that she was there again, in the most beautiful city in the world, a place where she had known the heights of happiness but where she had experienced seven months ago the depths of unhappiness when she had discovered how much Marco had deceived her.

The *vaporetto* slowed down, slid under the graceful shop-lined Rialto Bridge and sidled up to a landing stage, the most convenient stopping place for Piazza San Marco. Sandra followed Marco ashore and was soon walking beside him along the Calle Merceria, a twisting lane of luxury boutiques selling everything from expensive clothing and shoes to Venetian lace and glassware.

Long shadows slanted along the great Piazza San Marco, which was almost deserted on that cold, windy evening. There were no crowds of pigeon-feeders, no peanut vendors, no postcard-sellers and no gondoliers, either, coming forward to offer to take you gliding along darkened mysterious back canals, past high walls and closed doorways and under dainty arching bridges.

The clock in the famous Torre d'Orologio didn't strike as they walked under it and into the square because it strikes only on the hour. In front of them, the Campanile, severely austere, was a huge pointing finger looming against the sunset sky. On the left the Byzantine bulk of the domed and pinnacled Basilica San Marco glittered here and there with golden sparks struck from its mosaics by the last rays of the setting sun. Beside it, and in contrast with its overpowering splendour, the Doge's palace seemed like an elegant, sylph-like ghost, with its flat walls and lacy, arched *loggia*.

Brief glances were all Sandra could spare for the familiar and much-loved buildings as Marco marched

on past the colonnade of the classically designed
library and past the two monolithic columns, one
surmounted by the statue of the apostle, St Mark, and
the other by a winged lion. On to the San Marco
quayside they walked, where the high, decorated bows
of gondolas bobbed on violet-coloured, wind-rippled
water.

Turning right they walked past the yacht club over a
small bridge and stopped outside the front entrance of
the Palazzo Fontelli, a three-storeyed building con-
structed several centuries ago. They went up a flight of
shallow steps in the centre of five archways, through
double doors and into a thickly carpeted foyer. Marco
put down her case and pressed a button in a wall
beside a lift doorway.

The smooth glinting doors of the lift slid open and
they both entered the compartment. The doors slid
closed.

'I'll go up to Claire's apartment,' said Sandra. 'I'll
stay the night there.'

She stepped forward to press the button for the third
floor but he was there before her, pressing the button
for the second floor where his apartment was located.

'Claire's apartment is locked up,' he said. 'She
locked it when she left and gave the keys to Alfredo for
safe keeping. You remember Alfredo?'

She nodded. Alfredo Gerlini was the Fontelli family
lawyer and also legal adviser to the company.

'Luigi isn't there, then?' she queried.

'No, Luigi has retired and gone to farm in Sicily.
We have a new caretaker.'

'Oh.' She felt suddenly deflated and depressed.
Changes had happened during the past seven months,
changes she hadn't been told about. Suddenly she felt
very much an outsider. Perhaps she had always been

an outsider, even when she had lived in Venice with him. Though married to him she hadn't really been a part of the inner life of the city or of the company. She had just been Marco Morosini's wife.

The lift hummed to a stop and the doors slid open. Gesturing to her to go before him, Marco picked up her case and, after an initial hesitation, she stepped out into the hallway of the apartment that had been her home for a short time.

A Chinese carpet silenced her footsteps. From a bowl on a polished table set against a wall the scent of roses wafted up. Their petals were thick and velvety, ruby-coloured. Marco had often brought her a sheaf of such roses when he had returned from some business trip, and she wondered if he had had them arranged there especially to welcome her.

Through a wide archway she walked into the long living-room. The ceiling was high and fantastically decorated with plaster carvings and paintings. Three arched windows draped with golden brocade gave three framed views across the basin of San Marco to the island of San Giorgio floating on violet-tinted water, the *campanile* and dome of its old monastry complex glimmering with golden light against a rose-coloured sky.

But Sandra refused to be distracted by the beauty of the view or by the tasteful, luxurious furnishings of the room where all that was best in Italian design had been installed as befitted the home of one of the chief executives of Fontelli Enterprises. Turning, determined to face Marco now and to insist that he explain his mysterious behaviour, she found he wasn't in the room. Impatiently she marched back to the archway and into the hall.

'Marco?' she called.

'Here.' He appeared in a doorway further down the hall, the doorway to the master bedroom which she had once shared with him.

'I must talk to you. You must explain,' she began.

'I know, I know,' he interrupted her swiftly. 'But first you'll want to wash, change your clothes. Then we'll have a drink and later go out to dinner. At Mario's.' He named her favourite restaurant.

He came along the hall towards her. He had taken his sheepskin coat off and also his suit jacket. Undone at the collar, his stark white shirt emphasised the olive darkness of his skin. His long legs, clothed in fine worsted suiting, moved gracefully, and she stood mesmerised as she had often been in the past by his masculine beauty. He came right up to her, put his hands on her shoulders, smiled into her eyes and said quietly, 'I haven't greeted you properly, yet, *mia cara.* Welcome home.'

There was no time to turn her head to avoid his kiss. His firmly moulded lips came down on hers. The warm tip of his tongue flickered against the closed line of her mouth, and she swayed involuntarily against his tautly muscled body as a swift shiver of delight went through her. Then he raised his head. For a brief moment his eyes blazed smokily at her before his hands dropped from her shoulders and he stepped past her towards the living-room.

'I'll go and pour some wine,' he murmured.

One hand pressed against her lately plundered lips, Sandra struggled to control an upsurge of confused emotions and hurried in the opposite direction along the passage to the bedroom.

Nothing had changed in that room, which, with an extravagance that had shocked her at the time, Marco had had redesigned when they had married. Light from behind concealing panels slanted across the kitten-soft lilac carpet and shimmered on the turquoise-shot lilac silk spread of the sumptuous bed and the plump silk-covered ottomans at the foot of it. The Venetian blinds had been closed and the warmth and comfort of the room enfolded her like a lover's arms; like Marco's arms had enfolded her when they had slept together in the benign oriental-designed bed.

Welcome home, he had just said, and in this room she had shared with him she felt at home. It was her home. So why had she left it? Why had she run away from it and from him?

Evading the question this time, she took off her raincoat, laid it across a chair, unlocked her case, took out her toilet bag and lifted out the only dress she had packed. On her way to the clothes cupboard she stopped in mid-stride. What was she doing? She was behaving as if she intended to do exactly as Marco had told her to do, wash, change her clothes, prepare herself to go out to dinner with him.

Seeing her refelection hesitating in a long mirror, and not liking what she saw, she tossed her head and squared her jaw. Hanging her dress in the wardrobe didn't commit her to anything. It would be best if it hung for a while to let the creases fall out. She walked over to it.

About to push back one of the sliding doors, she hesitated again. Supposing she found another woman's clothes hanging in it? What would she do? Oh, she knew very well what she would do. She would drag them out and tear them apart. Then she would repack her case, put on her raincoat and storm out of the apartment just as she had last April.

Slowly and nervously she slid back the door. All that was hanging in that side of the closet was a black

négligé of her own. Marco had bought it for her and
had liked her to wear it. He had told her once that it
had made her look voluptuous. The sight of it now
brought back dozens of memories of being made love
to by Marco when she had been wearing it.

Moving jerkily, her face flushed, her heart racing,
she snatched a hanger from the rail, hung her dress on
it, put it back and closed the door quickly with a slam
because she didn't want to see the négligé any more.
She didn't want to be reminded of Marco's expertise
as a lover, nor titillated by memories of the way he had
always been able to find what gave her most sensual
pleasure.

She had managed without his kisses and the touch
of his hands for several months. Miles away from him,
she had learned not to yearn in the night for his
caresses, and she had grown a layer of ice over her
feelings where he was concerned. That ice, she
realised now, would be put to the test if she stayed in
this apartment tonight.

But she wasn't going to stay. She would leave at the
earliest opportunity. Picking up her toilet bag, she
stalked into the bathroom. Ceramic tiles covered the
walls and floor. They shimmered with the same
bluish-lilac hue of the bedroom. A sunken bath, a huge
oval mirror, a glass shower enclosure, plus plenty of
plants and piles of thick towels, combined together to
create a room of sybaritic luxury.

She sluiced her hands under piping hot water and
planned what she should do next. After she had got the
name of the hospital in Milan where Claire was, she
would leave. Marco couldn't stop her from leaving.
Only by using physical violence against her could he
stop her. The thought of him using his superior
strength to stop her from leaving made her gasp and

put a hand to her cheek as if it had been slapped. In the mirror she stared at herself with wide horrified eyes, thinking of all she had read about battered wives. Was this how it started? Did wives get battered when they refused to do what their husbands asked them to do?

'Hurry up.' His voice, deep and lazy, mocked her from the open doorway of the bathroom. 'The champagne will go flat if we don't drink it soon.'

She turned to look at him. Leaning casually against the door-jamb, hands in his trouser pockets, the hint of a smile curving his lips and warming his eyes, he was totally unlike the vicious, snarling monster she had imagined might use violence against her.

'Champagne?' she whispered. 'Why champagne? There's nothing to celebrate.'

'I think there is.' His smile faded and a frown took its place. 'What's the matter with you? Why are you looking at me like that?'

'How am I looking at you?' she stuttered, looking round for a towel.

'You were looking at me as if you were terrified of me.'

'You're mistaken,' she said as coolly as she could, drying her hands with her back to him.

'Sandra *cara*,' he murmured and she felt his hand on her shoulder.

'Please go,' she said quickly, trying to shake off his hand. Whatever else happened, she mustn't let him touch her. All kinds of strange things happened when he touched her. The ice began to melt rapidly. 'I . . . I haven't finished in here yet. Please go and shut the door after you. I . . . I'll join you in the lounge in a minute or two.'

To her relief he left. The door closed quietly. Her

eyes closed; her hands clenched at her sides, she drew a deep breath. Then, when she felt she had recovered control of her feelings, she washed her hands again. She was so confused she didn't know what she was doing, she thought indignantly. He confused her and he was right: she was afraid of him—not terrified, but afraid of his overpowering sexuality, his appeal to her senses ...

Stop thinking about it. Get on with what you've come to do. Find out where Claire is, go to see her and then go back to England. It's safer there than here.

Her face made up again and her hair brushed, she went along to the lounge. Marco was standing by the middle window, silhouetted against the sunset-flushed sky. Music played softly from the hi-fi system. Pavarotti singing 'O sole mio'. Romantic music for a romantic setting, a dusk-darkened room with the brightness of the Venetian sky outside and two tall Fontelli glasses, filled with champagne, winking on a a silver tray set on a low table before a velvet-covered loveseat. Oh yes, it was much safer in the flat in London than it was here. Dull, but safe.

Marco crossed the room to the low table. He picked up a glass and handed it to her.

'Thank you,' she said stiffly. 'I still think champagne is a bit ridiculous. There's nothing to celebrate. Quite the contrary. Claire is in hospital, badly hurt ...'

'Sit down,' he ordered, in his softest voice. 'Sit down here with me.' He sat on the loveseat.

Ignoring his request she sat down on a straight-backed winged chair on the other side of the table.

'You don't look very comfortable,' he remarked. 'And why didn't you change into something more attractive and relaxing?' The négligé, she guessed.

'That suit is awful,' he continued critically. 'Is it what all good librarians are wearing these days?'

From attentive husband and would-be lover, he had changed into a critical, derisive observer. He had always been amused by her choice of a career, believing that all female librarians were introspective, possibly sexually frustrated and with no knowledge of the world outside the books they looked after and read.

'I haven't changed because I'm not staying here for long,' she said, and even to her own ears she sounded prim. That he had noticed she knew by the way he grinned at her. She felt irritation with him rising in her again. More sharply, she said, 'Tell me where Claire is and how she is. I'm really very annoyed with this game you're playing. I can never understand why you're not more straightforward and truthful.'

Light glinted on his glass as he lifted it and drank from it and, glad that he hadn't bothered to make a toast, she sipped from her glass too, warning herself to drink slowly, remembering only too vividly how quickly champagne could go to her head making her reckless.

'Please tell me, Marco,' she pleaded, leaning forward and trying to impress upon him how sincerely concerned she was about Claire. 'How badly is she hurt?'

'You will see for yourself when you go to see her,' he said, smoothly evading the question, and she felt her temper beginning to flare up as she recognised that he was prevaricating. But, in time, she also recognised that nothing would be gained by losing her temper with him. She knew now, from past experience, that he possessed an enviable ability to turn the other cheek to her anger and to counter it with coolly reasoned arguments.

'I would like to go and see her,' she said firmly.

'Not tonight. You can't go tonight. By the time you reached Milan it would be too late,' he replied calmly.

'But I would be there, in the city, ready to go and see her tomorrow. I wish I knew why you're being so evasive. Last night you said I'd be sorry of I didn't come right away, so I thought she must have suffered fatal injuries and might die at any minute.' She drew in a long steadying breath, gripping her glass so hard she was in danger of breaking the slender stem between her fingers. 'Marco, she isn't, is she? She isn't dead?' she whispered anxiously.

'No. Of course not. How you do jump to conclusions,' he jeered. 'She's very much alive and was released from hospital this morning. I didn't know she had been released until it was too late to inform you. You were on your way here.' He stood up, walked over to her and held out a hand. 'More champagne? You see, we do have something to celebrate. Claire is alive and well.'

There was still some wine left in her glass but he took it anyway, and she sat staring into the shadows beyond the shafts of lamplight, hearing the clink of the champagne bottle against ice in the silver bucket.

She had flown all the way to Venice in answer to a summons to her mother's bedside, so she had believed. She had come expecting to find Claire helpless, possibly with a broken leg and a damaged face, possibly with brain damage, being intravenously fed, surrounded by life-supporting contraptions, unable to think, unable to act, unable to speak . . . oh, how her imagination had run riot, titillated no doubt by watching too many TV dramas.

Now she realised she had been duped. Marco had deceived her as he had before. She looked round at him. He was coming to her, offering her refilled glass. Taking it from him, she glared furiously at him. His eyebrows lifting in amused surprise, he turned away to sit on the loveseat again.

'You lied to me,' Sandra seethed, spitting the words out at him, forgetful of her resolution not to lose her temper. 'You lied to me last night on the phone. You said she ... she ...' She choked and had to pause to get her breath back. 'How could you?' she croaked accusingly. 'How could you lie about something like that? About an accident and fatal injuries?'

'I didn't do anything of the sort,' he retorted coldly. 'Claire was in a car accident and she was injured, but not fatally and not very seriously, so it seems now. I said nothing about fatal injuries. You jumped—with your great ability to do it—to another conclusion.'

'Only because you said I must come. You said that if I didn't come I would be sorry.' Feeling the need for courage to keep her anger going so that she could stand up to him, she drank more champagne quickly, uncomfortably aware that he could be right and that she had jumped to a conclusion.

'I didn't mean that you would be sorry about Claire if you didn't come,' he murmured expressionlessly, his eyes hidden by black-fringed lids.

'Then what did you mean?' she challenged.

'That is something you'll have to find out for yourself,' he parried suavely. 'I just passed on to you information about Claire because she asked me to. Then I asked you to come here.' His eyelids flicked up. He gave her a cold, hostile look. His face could have been sculpted from granite, it was so hard, the expression unyielding. 'You have been away long enough, Sandra. Six, almost seven, months is too long for a woman to stay away from her husband without good reason. It's also too long for a man to be separated from his wife. You have come. We will take it from there.' He spoke in cold clear tones and raised his glass. 'To our future together,' he toasted in a slightly warmer voice.

'Our future? Together?' She gasped incredulously. Had he gone mad? Or was he suffering from amnesia? Had he forgotten that when she had left this apartment last April she hadn't intended to return. *And I'm not coming back*. Those were the words she had flung at him, and she had kept her vow. There had been times when it had been hard, when she would have given anything to come rushing back to this lovely home he had created for her, to the warmth and strength of his arms, but she had stuck to her guns.

'Yes, our future together. We are still married and I see no reason why we shouldn't continue to be,' he said, in his softer, more persuasive manner.

'It's unbelievable,' she whispered, staring at him with wide eyes. 'Absolutely unbelievable.'

'What is?'

'Your ... your, well, your arrogance, I suppose I should call it; your barefaced effrontery in assuming that I've come to be with you. That I've come back to you because *you* asked me to come.'

'But didn't you come because I asked you?' he queried blandly. 'Did someone else ask you to come to Venice?'

'No!' She almost shouted the word at him. 'Oh, you know very well what I mean. I didn't come because you asked me to come. I came because you said I'd be sorry if I didn't come and I thought you meant I'd be sorry if I didn't come and Claire died. I didn't come to please you and I haven't come back to you.'

'I see.' He looked down at his empty glass, his lips twisting unpleasantly. 'So you think it's arrogant for a man to want his wife to return to him?' he said and gave her a swift under-browed glance, a flash-of-lightning glance which seemed to stab her. 'It's unfortunate that you think that way, because I don't agree with you. I believe I'm exercising my right as a husband to ask you to come back.' He put down his glass on the table, rose to his feet and came over to her. Leaning forward, he placed his hands on the arms of the chair in which she was sitting and looked at her, his eyes on a level with hers. Their glance, as warm as smoke, flitted over her face and came back to her eyes. 'Have you forgotten so soon, *mia cara*, the vows we made to each other until death parted us?'

Sandra's knees shook. It wasn't fair of him to take advantage of her in this way. He was wooing her with soft words and references to their runaway marriage which had been solemnised in a small village church in the Dolomites. Forcing her knees to co-operate, she began to push herself up out of the chair.

'Excuse me,' she said. 'I'd like to get up.'

He stood back and she rose, relieved that he didn't try to trap her in the chair any more. She walked over to the windows. She couldn't risk being close to him, she had discovered. He still had the power to make her dizzy with sexual desire. He seemed to possess a sort of black magic which, combining with the champagne, was having the effect of dispersing all her antagonism towards him.

'I seem to remember you didn't take those vows all that seriously,' she said. 'Making promises to me didn't stop you from continuing your . . . your affair with Lucia.'

There was silence behind her. She looked out of the window. The sky was dark blue now and a few stars glittered in it. Lights from the buildings on San Giorgio, reflected in the water of the San Marco basin, blazed like bursting fireworks.

'When I left Venice last April I was leaving you for good,' she went on and he didn't speak. 'For ever.' She spoke the words loudly and with emphasis, and waited for him to comment, but he remained silent, so she continued. 'You see, I'd found out what you're really like and I didn't want to live with you any more. I'd found out you're a cheat. I had no intention of coming back to you and that's why I haven't answered your letters, why I didn't want to see you when you came to London in August.'

He was silent again and she heard the clink of ice in the wine bucket as he lifted the bottle from it. She turned. He was pouring more champagne for himself.

'I don't believe you've heard a word I've said,' she declared, her voice shaking with anger.

He glanced sideways at her briefly, then back at his task of pouring champagne. When his glass was full again, he picked it up, sipped some wine and then, glass in hand, came over to her.

'You didn't say you were leaving for ever when you left,' he said smoothly. 'I've decided you've been away long enough. Now you've come back you're going to stay. I want you here, with me.'

'Oh, really, Marco,' she said with a little laugh, trying to cover up the strange spurt of fear she felt at his coldly possessive behaviour. 'How can you make me stay if I don't want to stay? This is the twentieth century, not the fourteenth. A man can't lock up his wife any more. He can't claim her as a possession, as one of his goods and chattels. You haven't got the message yet, have you? You still don't understand why I left you in April.'

'I understand you have some very weird ideas about marriage,' he retorted. 'And I know why you left. You left because you'd been shaken out of that romantic dream in which you had been living, a dream in which I starred as a rich prince who had chosen you to be his bride to live happily ever after. You left because you found out suddenly that I'm human after all, and that you weren't the only woman I'd made love to during my life.' His glance swept over her critically and he looked at his watch. 'We dine at eight-thirty,' he added matter-of-factly. 'You have more than two hours to attend to your appearance. I hope you've brought a decent dress with you, something better than that dowdy suit you're wearing.'

'I dress to please myself, not you,' she retorted.

'That's obvious,' he sneered. 'Your standards aren't very high if that suit pleases you.'

'It's the latest style,' she muttered, looking down at the long loose jacket and the even longer skirt. She had to admit they looked droopy, sagging on her slim figure.

'That doesn't mean that it's the best style for you,' he argued. 'On you it looks like someone else's cast off-rags. Now, do you or don't you have something better to wear?'

'Something which you wouldn't mind *your* wife being seen in, I suppose you mean?' She tilted her chin at him.

'I do.' He finished his wine and put the glass down.

'We'll never agree on this,' she seethed. 'I'm not your property. I'm not something you own and can take out to show off to your friends. Marco, will you please listen to me.' He had turned away from her with a shrug and had begun to walk out of the room so she had to hurry after him. In the archway, he stopped, turned to look at her, his lips curling, his slanted glance cold.

'I have no wish to listen to such drivel,' he said.

'It's not drivel!' she gasped. her temper flaring again. 'It's what any free, independent woman thinks and believes. Oh, I know why you married me . . .'

'If you do, why did you leave me?' he cut in, sharp as a rapier.

'Because I found out you'd tricked me. You pretended you married me because you loved me, but all the time you were thinking how advantageous it would be to be married to the daughter of the chairperson of Fontelli's. And also you wanted a wife who would make your colleagues and friends envious of you. That's why you always want me to dress up!' She paused to draw breath, then burst out, 'For you, marrying me was like buying a new sports car or a new speedboat.'

But Sandra's outburst didn't seem to hurt him. Nothing she did or said ever seemed to get through his tough armour of worldliness. Marco was much more sophisticated than she would ever be, and he had been using his wits to plot and scheme his way in business for more than half her life. Now he was looking at her with a rather pitying expression that made her want to scream and rant at him even more.

'You're very amusing,' he drawled, his smile half sweet and half malicious. 'But you read too much and believe everything you read, then apply it to your own situation. I've never thought of you as a piece of property that I own. I've always thought of you as an attractive and often lovable woman.'

'There, you see,' she pounced. 'You don't think of me as a *person*. You think of me as a woman.'

'So what's wrong with that?' he retorted. 'I'm a man and I'm not interested in going to bed with a *person*. I married you because I believed you to be all woman, not one of those persons who aren't at all sure what gender they are.' His voice rasped with disgust. 'But it's possible I made a mistake,' he went on more slowly, looking suddenly weary. 'Perhaps I expected too much of you. That's one reason why I asked you to come here so we can discuss the situation and reach some conclusion together, not jump to one. Will you agree to stay here a few days while we work something out?'

It sounded all very cold and dry, not a bit romantic, thought Sandra, all the fire in her dying down. His realistic assessment of the situation was threatening to defeat her. She wished she could needle him into losing his temper as he could make her lose hers.

'But what about Claire? I came to see her,' she complained.

'I promise I'll take you to see her as soon as we've talked and made some arrangement, come to some agreement,' he said.

'How do I know you'll keep your promise?' she sniped bitterly.

'You don't.' Again he smiled tauntingly at her. 'Meanwhile, would you like to talk to Claire? I have a phone number I can call. Would that please you? Then you can ask her yourself if she is all right.'

'Yes. I would like to speak to her.' All her irritation had gone.

'Then go and sit down, have another glass of wine while I put the call through for you. It'll be long

CHAPTER THREE

THE study was the most relaxed room in the apartment. Books and magazines were scattered about and chairs were deep and comfortable. Sandra had spent many hours in it with Marco, some of the happiest she had ever known during their short marriage. Where had they gone, those happy times, and would they ever come again?

She arrived in the room too late to hear the number he was phoning. She heard only that he was making a personal call to Claire and then he hung up.

'The operator will call back when she has contacted Claire,' he explained. Again, briefly and disparagingly, his glance swept over her. 'I asked you if you had something else to wear but you didn't answer. Do you? Have you brought a dress suitable for dining out in?'

'Supposing I said I hadn't. What would you do?' she challenged.

'Take you out to buy one. The stores are still open.' Sitting with one hip on the corner of the desk he was relaxed and unperturbed. Didn't anything ever disconcert him?

'I have a dress with me,' she said quickly. She didn't want him escorting her from boutique to boutique until *he* found a dress *he* liked and *he* would pay for. That would give him too much of an advantage over her, more than he had already.

The phone rang. Marco slid off the desk.

'You take it,' he said. 'I'm going to shower and to

change. I'm sure you wish your conversation with Claire to be private.'

With that final jibe he left the room and, knowing full well he could listen to any conversation she might have with Claire on the extension phone in the bedroom, Sandra picked up the receiver and spoke into it. The operator informed her that the party she had been calling was on the line and then she heard Claire's voice, pleasant and beautifully modulated.

'Sandra? Is it really you, darling? How nice of you to phone. Where are you?'

'In Venice. At the *palazzo*. Marco phoned me last night, said you'd been in a car accident and that you were asking for me. He insisted that I fly here this morning. I thought you were in hospital in Mestre but now he tells me that the accident happened near Milan. Oh, Claire, are you really all right?'

'I've felt better, darling. But nothing was broken, thank God. I suffered a little from shock and whiplash and was allowed to leave hospital this morning.' There was a little pause and then Claire said warm and approvingly, 'It's good to hear that you and Marco are together again . . .'

'But we're not. We're not,' Sandra interrupted hastily. 'I wouldn't be here, I wouldn't have come if I hadn't thought you were seriously injured.'

'Wouldn't you?' The approval had gone from the pleasant voice. Now Claire sounded cooler, distant, as if she were backing away from something nasty that she didn't want to know about. 'But why not? You and Marco are married to each other, so you should be together. Frankly, darling, I can't understand why you've stayed away from him for so long. Or, for that matter, why you went away to England in the first place. It's a very dangerous thing for a woman to do, you know, to leave her husband on his own for so long. He could have got into all kinds of mischief while you've been away. With other women, I mean. If you had consulted me in April before you left I would have advised you quite strongly not to stay away too long. I've known Marco longer than I've known you and he has never been short of female companionship for long. To tell the truth, darling, even though you're my daughter I was rather surprised when he chose to marry you. He could have had his pick of many lovely and well-connected—socially, I mean—women . . .'

'But you weren't here,' Sandra complained loudly, knowing that if she didn't interrupt Claire would go on and on in the same vein for a while and then suddenly say they had talked long enough and hang up. 'You were away last April. And it was partly because of another woman that I left.'

'What other woman?' Claire demanded sharply, interested at last.

'I can't tell you over the phone. Claire, where are you? I'd like to come and see you. That's why I've come to Italy, to see you. I've only a few days off from work . . .'

'And that's another thing!' Claire's turn to interrupt and her tone was not most disapproving. 'Why did you go back to work? You've no need to earn money. You have plenty of your own . . .'

'Not my own, Claire. Marco's . . .'

'I was sure he had made you a generous allowance,' said Claire. 'You don't need to work.'

'Please, Claire. I can't discuss this now. Where are you? Please tell me and I'll come and see you tomorrow. Joan is quite worried about you, too. She asked me to phone her as soon as I was satisfied you're all right and not badly hurt.'

There was a short silence. Sandra thought she could hear Claire speaking to someone else but could not make out what she was actually saying. Then she spoke into the phone again.

'Sandra?'

'Yes?'

'I'd really rather not tell you where I am and I don't want you to come and see me tomorrow. Perhaps next week . . .'

'But I won't be in Italy next week. I'll have to return to London on Sunday. I've only a few days' leave.'

'If you've any sense you'll stay on with Marco,' said Claire, sharp again. 'I'm sorry, darling. You'll just have to come back next spring to see me, if you're not going to stay. I might . . . just might, be in Venice then. And now I must go. We're going out to dinner and I must change. Goodbye, darling, and thanks for phoning me and being so concerned about me. Lovely to hear from you.'

'Claire, wait!' Sandra found she was shouting into the phone, shouting into a hollow silence. Claire had hung up.

Irritation flared through her and she crashed the receiver down on the rest, swore vigorously and flung the pen she had been doodling with across the room. For the first time since she had met Claire she realised how selfish her natural mother was; how Claire always put herself first. Claire wasn't a *natural* mother. She was an *unnatural* mother. She was a mother without any natural maternal instincts, who had preferred to give up her only child to live in luxury with a man who hadn't wanted to be a stepfather.

About to leave the room Sandra had a sudden idea. Finding another pen in the holder on the desk she picked up the receiver and dialled for an operator.

Then in her slow, careful Italian, she asked for the area code and number of the phone to which she had just been connected, explaining that someone else had made the initial call for her and she wasn't sure of the number but wanted to call it again and speak personally to Claire Fontelli. The operator complied with her request, gave her the number which she wrote down on a pad and then told her to put down the receiver. After a few moments the phone rang again. The operator told her that there was no answer from the number she had called. She then asked if the operator knew which district had such an area code. The operator said the code number was for a district near Genoa. Claire was still in Italy.

What was going on? What game were Claire and Marco playing? Why didn't Claire want her to visit tomorrow? She could easily get to the Riviera area near Genoa. And who was Claire staying with over there? With the piece of paper on which she had written Claire's phone number clutched in her hand, Sandra left the study and went along to the master bedroom determined to confront Marco, tell him she knew where Claire was but not exactly the place she was staying in and to demand he tell her Claire's address.

He wasn't in the bedroom, and without considering how her behaviour might look to him she marched over to the bathroom door, opened it and walked straight in just as Marco, his bare skin glistening with drops of water, his hair hanging in wet fronds over his forehead, stepped out of the shower. Confronted with his powerful yet symmetrical naked body, she pulled up short, all that she intended to say forgotten for a few moments. He, it seemed, was not as nonplussed as she was.

'*Carissima*,' he purred, a smile tilting his lips as he advanced on her and he continued in Italian. He had always made love to her in that language. 'This is an unexpected pleasure. Why didn't you say you wish to take a shower with me? I would have waited for you.'

'I don't . . . I didn't come . . . I've no wish . . .' she stammered in English, her Italian unequal to the occasion, and although she backed away from him her glance seemed to be glued to his damp body and she had to clench her hands at her sides to stop them from reaching out to him. She wanted so much to feel him again, to touch him everywhere.

'But I think you should take your clothes off first,' he said still advancing. 'Let me help you.'

His skin gleamed with a golden sheen under the electric light and the black hairs on his broad chest glittered with diamond drops of water. He smelt exotic from the soap he had used—sandalwood she thought—and when he stepped closer to her her senses seemed to reel from inhaling it. He took hold of one end of the silk tie of her ivory-coloured blouse and pulled it to undo the bow.

Finding his scented nakedness too much for her, she stepped back again and the bow slipped undone. Grabbing hold of the long wide ribbon of silk, she pulled it from his wet fingers and, turning quickly, fled from the bathroom, closing the door behind her.

For a moment she hesitated, breathing hard, trying to regain her equilibrium, then she went over to the dressing-table to look in the mirror while she retied the bow of her blouse. Bewildered, she stared at the three images of herself in the triple mirror. Her cheeks were flushed pink, her eyes were sparkling and her ruffled hair seemed to shoot with red sparks. With shaking fingers she started to tie the bow, wondering when her heart would stop beating so madly, wondering too, what she would do if she couldn't contain and suppress the sexual excitement her abrupt encounter with Marco in the bathroom had roused. She hadn't taken into account that she might want him once she was with him again, she thought wryly, and for the first time she understood why she was afraid of him. She wasn't really afraid of him as a person. She was afraid of her own physical responses to his masculine attractions; afraid of her own desires.

'So what did you burst into the bathroom for if it wasn't to share a shower with me?' asked Marco tauntingly.

He appeared in the three mirrors behind her. He had draped a towel around his hips, leaving his chest and shoulders bare, and his drying hair was brushed back from his forehead behind his ears. His light eyes glinted wickedly between their black lashes; he was a dark, devilish figure against which her own bright colouring glowed fierily. He put his hands lightly on her shoulders and she stiffened immediately and defensively.

'Don't touch me. Take your hands off me,' she said tautly.

'Why?' His reflected face mocked her, the black eyebrows slanting satirically, the firm lips curving sensually. 'Are you afraid of what happens to you when I touch you?' he asked, guessing far too accurately at her feelings.

'No, I'm not,' she lied emphatically. 'How conceited you are to think you can ... you can ...'

'Turn you on?' he suggested with a grin. 'But I can,

mia cara, I always could. That's why you married me. Remember?'

His hands slipped down and across the top of her chest until they rested just below her throat. Long, lean and olive-skinned, the fingers sprinkled with dark hairs, they contrasted threateningly with her white skin, two tensile weapons designed to assault her. They had only to slide upwards a little and they would cut off her breath, she thought wildly. They could throttle her. Her heart pounding in her ears, she made no attempt to free herself, afraid that if she did she might set off some violent reaction in him.

'Please let me go,' she whispered.

For answer he tipped his head forward. She saw the reflection of his drying hair springing up, the jet blackness of it making the parting seem startlingly white. Then his lips were hot against the side of her neck. The caress was familiar, the kiss that had always been a prelude to their lovemaking. It both seared and seduced, sending messages of white-hot desire flickering through her.

'No, Marco, no,' she moaned, her hands on his to pull them away, although her body ignored the direction of her will and behaved contrarily, swaying back against his hard pulsing body. Her eyes closed as a spinning blackness took over her mind. Beneath the silk of her blouse her breasts lifted and hardened. 'You can't treat me like this, as if I am ...'

'As if you are my wife?' he whispered in her left ear. 'But you are my wife.'

His hands on her shoulders again he spun her round as if she were a puppet without muscle, without control over the movements of her own body.

'Now you're here I intend to make the most of your visit,' he murmured, his eyes sultry with desire.

'No.' Hands against his bare chest she pushed. 'Not yet. You promised we would discuss the situation first.'

'Not first. Later. After,' he mocked with the glint of a smile. 'To hell with discussion.'

He possessed her mouth in a hard, brutal kiss that cut off any further protest on her part. Ruthlessly his lips parted hers and a swimming giddiness spun her round and round. Before she knew what she was doing she was kissing him back, fondling his bare chest, feeling again the erotic sensations spreading through her like hot flames; aroused by the scents of his skin and hair, the touch of his fingertips and the taste of his mouth.

'I want you and I must have you, Sandra *mia*. Now,' he growled thickly. 'But first this awful suit must come off.'

As he raised his hands to strip the jacket from her, she staggered on shaking legs away from him. But she was too slow. He reached out one long arm and caught her around the waist, lifted her easily and dumped her down on the silken bed amongst plump cushions, and he was there immediately beside her, the towel gone. Dark and menacing, he leaned over her, eyes smoky with lust, hands pulling at the fastenings of her blouse.

'Marco, listen. Please. I'll never forgive you for this. If you force me I'll . . .'

'No force will be needed, sweetheart. You'll see. It never has been needed between you and me. It comes to us naturally because we both want each other.'

Protest was swallowed again in the heat of his mouth. His lips stroked and wooed hers while his fingers strayed amongst the thickness of her hair, and stroked her throat before sliding inevitably down to her breasts. Gently and expertly he stroked away her blouse while keeping her quiet with his kiss. Once more the darkness invaded her mind, a whirling darkness splintered with flame-coloured sparks and, hardly aware of what she was doing, she helped him to remove the rest of her clothing.

Then, groaning helplessly as her body betrayed her, lifting involuntarily to his touch, she flung her arms around him and pulled him down on top of her. Under his heavenly, much-missed weight she was buried and almost smothered as his lips and hands and the subtle movements of his body incited her to share with him the climax of passion. She could hardly breathe. But, oh, she could feel, inside and out. She could feel the heat and throb of his passion and the delicious needle-pricks of her own exquisitely excited nerves.

Suddenly she was shooting upwards out of the darkness. Up and up she went to explode in a white blinding light, and they were both laughing and groaning, the sounds stifled against skin and hair and he was whispering triumphantly, 'Nothing forced about that, *cara mia*.'

Stunned into a sort of stupor Sandra lay limply on the bed for a while, knowing vaguely that Marco had rolled away from her, but too lax and limp to open her eyes to see where he was. Gradually she became aware that what she had been afraid of happening if she was in too close contact with him had happened. Once again he had conquered her physically, had led her into the depths of desire, as if their physical union was all that mattered, as if it would solve the problems that had led to their separation.

Far away, coming through the languorous haziness that engulfed her, she thought she heard voices. She raised heavy eyelids, turned her head. Marco wasn't beside her. He had gone, leaving her alone on the chaos of the bed. She sat up. In the soft lighting she could see her clothes strewn about the floor, wherever they had fallen after Marco had tossed them aside. A little smile, a purely feminine smile, curved her lips and she knew a moment of secret triumph. Marco had been right. It had been natural and enjoyable, nothing forced. They had both wanted, *needed* it.

But there were definitely other people in the apartment—a man and a woman. She could hear the rise and fall of their voices and the deep murmur of Marco's voice. They must have arrived without her hearing them. She had been too steeped in the languor induced by satisfaction. Her lips quirked again into a smile but this time it was wry. Might as well face facts. She had been too stunned and shaken by her complete capitulation to Marco's lovemaking to notice anything else, and now the lovely joyous feeling she had experienced immediately after their reunion was being pushed out by a feeling of resentment because he was still able to rouse in her such a passionate response.

She pushed her hair back from her forehead and shrugged. No point in regrets; the deed was done. But her mind was still her own, and now it was warning her that it would be dangerous for her to stay with him any longer. As soon as she could she would leave. Nothing had changed just because they had made love. He still regarded her as a possession to be shown off to his friends and business colleagues, as a doll to dress up in clothes he liked. He still didn't understand her or regard her as a person in her own right.

And then there was Lucia.

Quickly, she left the bed and went into the bathroom. When she had showered she changed into the dress she had hung in the wardrobe. Made of emerald-green velvet and bought for her last Christmas by Marco, it clung to her figure, and the deep V of the neck showed the cleft between her breasts. The sleeves were long and tight-fitting, the waist was belted and the skirt was flared, the hem just below the knees. It annoyed her to have to admit that the colour and style of the dress played up her white skin, the burnished reddish-brown of her hair, and accentuated the green flecks in her eyes, and it annoyed her that she had to wear it, because Marco had bought it for her, but it was easy to pack and to wear.

She slipped her feet into high-heeled black shoes, arranged a long loop of pearls around her neck, again wishing that Marco hadn't given them to her. If they were going out she would have to wear the raincoat she had brought with her over her dress instead of a coat, but since it was stylishly cut from smooth grey gaberdine it looked, she thought, quite smart. What Marco's opinion would be of it, she daredn't think.

She was picking up her discarded suit and blouse from the floor when Marco came back into the room. He had obviously dressed hurriedly in a clean white shirt and the well-cut trousers of another suit, dark grey with a fine, dark red line woven into it. His hair was still ruffled from the touch of her hands and his eyes looked sleepy. He gave her a lazily intimate smile as he looked her over.

'I'm sorry I had to leave you,' he said coming over to her. 'You look more like *my* Sandra, now,' he added softly and bending swiftly brushed her lips with his, an act of such flagrant possession that she stepped back from him quickly. 'It was, good, very good. We must do it again. Later, tonight,' he added with a wickedly importunate glance that flicked from her lips to her partially revealed breasts.

'Not if I can help it,' she retorted, but there was no conviction in her voice. It wobbled weakly and she couldn't take her eyes away from his lips. 'Did . . . did I hear voices?' she managed to ask, finding safety in the mundane.

'You did.'

Stepping past her he went over to his side of the wardrobe, slid open a door, took a jacket from the hanger and slipped it on. Selecting a tie from a rack of them, he went over to the dressing-table to watch himself knot his tie. Sandra watched too, fascinated by the deft movements of his hands, her body tingling unexpectedly at the memory of their touch, so recently experienced.

'Who is here?' she demanded.

'Some relatives of mine from the States,' he replied, taking up a brush to smooth his hair. 'They'll be dining with us, and I invited them to call in on their way to the restaurant to have a drink with us and to meet you.'

'You were so sure I'd be here?' she exclaimed. In the three mirrors their eyes met, hers more green than grey, reflecting the colour of the dress, sparkling like emeralds.

'I was sure,' Marco said with aggravating arrogance as, fastening the long-lapelled, elegant, double-breasted jacket of his suit, he turned to face her. 'I knew you'd come when you heard about Claire,' he said mockingly.

'Then you did trick me,' she cried.

'But aren't you glad I did?' he taunted. 'Just think what you'd have missed if you hadn't come.' He gestured towards the tumbled silk of the bed his grin flashing tormentingly. 'Don't take it so seriously, my love,' he whispered, taking hold of her arm and urging her towards the door. 'Come, now. Come and meet them.'

Nothing had changed, she thought as they walked along the hallway. Her leaving in April had done no damage to his ego. It hadn't even dented it. He still thought of her as his possession. True, he talked often of love to her; after all, he was partly Italian. Once she had believed him. But now she knew the feeling didn't go deeply with him. For him, love was nine-tenths physical. He loved where he found sexual satisfaction. The other tenth of love was possession. He loved what he owned.

'Here she is,' he announced, and there was no mistaking the note of triumph in his voice as they walked into the lounge. 'My wife, Sandra.' Not, this is Sandra, but my wife. Sandra gritted her teeth. '*Cara*,' he went on. 'I'd like you to meet Liza and Ian Morison.'

The two people, who were standing close to each other studying an original painting by Picasso, another of Marco's prize possessions, turned when Marco made his announcement. The woman was tall and shapely and about fifty-five years of age. She was dressed simply in black. Her hair was jet-black too, save for one streak of silver, and her features were finely chiselled, almost familiar. From under arching eyebrows her dark eyes regarded Sandra with a critical interest that made Sandra glad she had brought the green dress and changed into it.

'At last we meet,' said Liza Morison. 'I've heard much about you.' She spoke English with an American twang, and came forward holding out her right hand to Sandra.

Wondering whether to lie and say she had heard

much about Liza Morison, Sandra took the out-
stretched hand, muttering something about being
pleased to meet her.

'I've been looking forward to this meeting too,' said
Ian Morison, also coming across to shake hands. A
little older than Liza, Sandra judged, he had light grey
eyes set under bristling bronze eyebrows and he spoke
with just the slightest suggestion of a Scottish accent.
His lean hand gripped hers tightly and his eyes
twinkled. 'Am I allowed to kiss you?' he asked. 'After
all you are my only niece-in-law.'

Suppressing her surprise on learning that he was
Marco's uncle, Sandra managed a smile and offered
her cheek to Ian's avuncular peck. She muttered
something polite again while secretly and viciously
calling Marco names for having played yet another
trick on her, with this offbeat introduction to a near
relative of his about whom he had told her nothing.

Morison. Morosini. She mused on the similarity of
the two names as they sat drinking champagne and
chattering about this and that. She glanced stealthily
at Ian Morison. Thinning sandy hair, a long-jawed
face and those frosty deep-set grey eyes, so similar to
Marco's. Ian looked Scottish as well as sounding
Scottish, and the name Morison was a common one in
Scotland. Morison's Workshops. Of course. That was
why it was familiar to her. Only last night she and
Thea had been talking about Morison's silver and
pewter ware. And Ian Morison's brother must be
Marco's father. Why had no one ever told her that?
Why hadn't Marco?

Her glance swerved to Liza, and she surprised the
woman watching her. Caught staring openly, Liza was
too much a woman of the world to be embarrassed.
She smiled and leaning forward whispered, 'Is there a

mirror where I could see myself, please? I have a feeling I've put on too much make-up. Ian was so excited about coming to meet you that he rushed me.'

'Come to the bedroom,' suggested Sandra, and rose to her feet.

They excused themselves to the two men, who seemed to be deep in conversation about Fontelli Enterprises in the United States and went along the passage to the master bedroom. As soon as they entered the room Liza turned to Sandra with a mishievous little grin.

'It wasn't much of a ruse to get you to myself for a few minutes, but it was all I could think of,' she said. 'I don't wear much make-up at all. Didn't you notice?'

'No, I didn't,' said Sandra, gazing at Liza's soft olive-tinted cheeks and wondering why it was that people were always tricking her.

'You were looking so bewildered,' Liza went on as she sat down on one of the silk-covered ottomans at the foot of the bed. She glanced around the room. 'This is really something. Very Byzantine. Not your choice I suspect, but Marco's. We Venetians have a lot that is Moorish or Arabic in our make-up as well, of course, some hints of more northern ancestors. We're a mixed-up lot. Maybe that's why we're so devious.' She glanced at Sandra again. 'You've really been left in the dark about us, about me and Ian, I mean, haven't you? You knew nothing about us until you were introduced to us just now. Am I right?'

'Yes, you are,' sighed Sandra, sinking down in an armchair. 'Marco didn't tell me you were here in Venice or that you would be dining with us until you arrived. I've only just come from England and there hasn't been much time . . .'

'So Marco was telling us,' Liza interrupted swiftly.

'You've been there for several months, haven't you? Visiting relatives, he said.' Liza's mobile eyebrows twitched sardonically as if she hadn't believed a word Marco had said. 'But he should have warned you he was expecting us this evening and that Ian is his uncle. He's alway's been very secretive, and we didn't know he had married you until last April. You're Claire's daughter, I believe?'

'Yes.'

'And that's something else we didn't know. I was very surprised to learn she had a daughter. She kept very quiet about you all the years she was married to Francesco. I wonder if he knew about you.'

'Yes, he did.' Sensing that Liza was annoyed because she hadn't known sooner that Claire Fontelli had a daughter, Sandra decided to change the direction of the conversation slightly.

'I know you're right about Marco being secretive. He's never told me anything about his parents and I've always assumed him to be connected with the old Venetian family of Morosini,' she said.

'Ah, so you've noticed the similarity between Morison and Morosini,' said Liza with a laugh. 'Did you think he's a descendant of one of the doges of Venice, Francesco Morosini? How amusing. Marco's last name was once Morison, but when he came to live in Venice my brother suggested it be changed to Morosini, perhaps thinking of the connection to the one-time doge that might be made. He was full of tricks, too.' Liza smiled complacently, as if being tricky was something admirable.

'Your brother?' queried Sandra who, now she had found someone to give her some information about

Marco's family, was determined to find out as much as she could.

'Francesco.' Liza gave another of her infectious laughs. 'Oh, didn't you know that either? I thought that Claire might have mentioned it to you. I'm a Fontelli, Francesco's younger sister.'

'So that's why there's something familiar about you,' exclaimed Sandra. 'I can see a resemblance in your face to a photograph Claire has of the count.'

'I'm glad you think I resemble him. He was a very handsome man.'

'I suppose you met Marco's uncle, Ian, when Fontelli's took over the Morison workshops in Scotland,' murmured Sandra.

'Yes, I did. Francesco took quite a fancy to Ian and so did I. After we were married, Ian took over the management of Fontelli Enterprises in the States and we went to live in New York. We've lived there ever since. Marco used to stay with us often when he was studying for his MBA. He and my daughter have always been very close, very good friends.'

'What about Marco's father? Does he still live in Scotland and does he still manage the workshops?' asked Sandra. 'I can't help wondering why Marco hasn't told me about him or why he's never come to visit us.'

'Marco's father?' queried Liza sharply. 'Whoever are you talking about?'

'I suppose I'm talking about Ian's brother, if Ian is really Marco's uncle,' said Sandra equally sharp.

'Ian is really Marco's uncle but not because his brother is or was Marco's father. Ian's brother is much younger than he is and is a teacher of painting at a Scottish college of art. Hasn't Marco ever told you anything about his mother?'

'No. He's told me nothing.'

'It's no wonder that you're flummoxed, as you say in English. Marco's mother was Ian's sister.'

'Then his name isn't Morison.'

'Oh, yes, it is. His mother was Isabel Morison and when he was born he was registered under her family name. Possibly that is why he has never told you about her. Perhaps he thinks you wouldn't approve if you knew he was born out of wedlock,' suggested Liza.

Sandra was silent. She was thinking that Marco's arrival in the world was very like her own.

'Perhaps I've told you too much,' said Liza softly.

'Oh, no. I'm glad you have.' Sandra looked up to find the dark eyes watching her narrowly again. 'Did you know her? Isabel Morison, I mean?'

'No. She had died years before I met Ian. She was an artist too, or at least training to be one when she visited Italy, met a man and fell in love with him. It happens all the time, as you know. It happened to you. Something in the air. Or something about Italians.' Liza laughed and shrugged her shoulders. 'Anyway, when she went back to Scotland she found she was pregnant. She told her parents and decided to keep the baby. Something went wrong at the birth, I'm not sure what. It seems she was never very strong. She died but the baby survived. Her parents adopted him and christened him Mark.'

'Didn't she ever tell them who the father was? Did she contact him?'

'No, never, to my knowledge. She was a very independent young woman, very proud. Something like you, perhaps? The man, whoever he was, had deceived her, had seduced her pretending he loved her, but she was going to take the responsibilty for her own actions. She left him when she found he had deceived her and had her revenge on him by not telling him about the baby, although, of course, it's possible he wouldn't have cared about it anyway. Some men are like that.' Liza shrugged indifferently and rose to her feet. 'I think it's time we went to the restaurant, don't you? Marco said eight thirty and it's now ten past eight. I'm really glad I've had this little talk with you, and I hope you don't feel quite so much in the dark, now.'

'In the dark about what?' asked Marco sharply from the doorway and whirling to face him, Sandra wondered how long he had been standing there listening.

'I've just been filling Sandra in on how you come to be related to Ian. Now she knows, and not before time,' said Liza smoothly as she walked past him. She reached up and patted his cheek affectionately. 'It was really too bad of you not to tell her, you know. She must be wondering now in what other ways you've deceived her.'

Liza went on out of the room. Taking her raincoat from her, Marco held it for Sandra to slip into the sleeves.

'Have you felt in the dark about me?' he enquired.

'Yes, I have,' she replied stiffly, picking up her handbag and slipping it over her arm.

'Then tell me about it as we walk to Mario's,' he said, and they left the room together.

CHAPTER FOUR

THEY walked across the shadowy Piazza San Marco, under the clock tower with its two figures of Moors standing arrested, waiting to toll the bell on the next hour. The damp paving of the Calle Merceria shimmered with reflected light slanting out from the windows of shops that were just closing.

Sandra walked with Marco. Her right arm was linked in his left one. Or rather it was trapped by him, she thought, because he had taken hold of her right hand with his right one and had pulled it through the crook of his arm and then had kept hold of her hand in a tight grip. They walked ahead of Liza and Ian, weaving their way through the people who were window shopping, on their way home from shopping or just out for the usual evening stroll.

'Why didn't you ever tell me about Ian or about your mother?' Sandra whispered to Marco as soon as they were far enough ahead of Liza and Ian not to be overheard.

'You didn't ask. Not once did you ever ask me about any family I might have, so I gathered you weren't interested,' he replied. 'I suppose Liza told you about how my grandparents adopted me.'

'Yes. You should have told me yourself. I felt very foolish just now having to admit to Liza I'd never heard about Ian or her or any other relative of yours.'

'You didn't tell me you're Claire's daughter,' he retorted, 'you kept me in the dark, too. But then if I remember rightly neither of us was very much

73

interested in the other's family tree.' There was a
sarcastic edge to his voice. 'We were much more
interested in sleeping together.'

'I didn't tell you I'm Claire's daughter because she
asked me not to tell anyone,' she defended herself. 'I
wanted to tell you but she asked me not to. Anyway,
you knew I was her daughter. You'd found out
somehow. Or you'd guessed. That's why you suddenly
started to show an interest in me and that was why you
asked me to marry you. You wanted to be related to
the chairperson of the company, the one who owned
more than fifty per cent of the shares.'

He didn't say anything. He didn't deny her
accusation and she felt a sense of deep disappointment. If he'd denied her accusation when she had first
made it last April she wouldn't have left him. It had
been his silence on the subject, combined with his
silence on the matter of Lucia, that had disillusioned
her. And now he wasn't saying anything again in
defence of himself.

The Calle Merceria took a turn to the right. Directly
in front of them was a small humped-back bridge over
a canal. Marco stopped so she had to stop too. He
looked back to make sure Liza and Ian could see
which direction he was going to take, then urged
Sandra across the bridge. Turning left, they walked
along a narrow path beside the light-reflecting canal,
passing on their right hand the closed doorways and
grille-fronted windows of old high buildings, the backs
of shops and apartment dwellings that fronted on to
another wider street.

They met no people on that narrow path and all was
quiet except for the click of Sandra's high heels on the
pavement and the occasional gurgle of water against a
stone wall. At one point, feeling her hand going numb

in his tight grip, Sandra tried to slide her arm from under his but he wouldn't let go.

'I don't want to walk arm in arm with you,' she muttered.

'It looks better if we do,' he said.

'Better to whom?' she demanded trying again to twist her hand free of his.

'To them.' He jerked his head back in the direction of the couple behind them. 'I don't want them to suspect there is anything wrong with our marriage.'

'Wrong? Oh, you mean you don't want them to guess that our marriage is on the rocks and about to break up at any minute,' she jeered. 'You haven't changed, ' she went on bitterly. 'You're still thinking of how you and anything you do looks to other people. You're still a master of deceit, a pretender. And I don't want to be an accomplice in your trickery. I don't want to walk arm in arm with you. Let go.' She tried again to break free of him.

'I admit to tricking you to come back to Venice so that you'd be here for this dinner we're going to, but that isn't the only reason I wanted you to come back; surely I convinced you on the bed in the apartment an hour ago that I wanted you to come back because I want you.' He stopped abruptly, as she continued to try to pull her hand free of his, and swung round on her. In the faint light coming from a lamp above a doorway she saw his eyes flash angrily and the glint of his teeth as he spoke. 'For God's sake,' he growled savagely. 'Can't you behave in a civilised way for once? Can't you control your temper?'

'*Ouch*!' She winced as his hand threatened to crush her fingers to a pulp. He was doing what she had feared. He was using his superior strength to intimidate her. She could hear Liza's and Ian's footsteps approaching. Glaring up at Marco's shadowed face she whispered, 'All right. You can stop hurting me and start behaving in a civilised way yourself. I'll behave for a short while. I'll be polite and submissive while we're with them. But I don't like it. I don't like the deception and the pretence which you call behaving in a civilised way. I don't call it that. I call it intrigue. I like to be honest and open . . .'

'You like to be perverse,' he retorted blightingly and, still holding her hand, though not as tightly, he strode on; she could do nothing else but go with him, almost running to keep up with him. 'You like to go out of your way to irritate me,' he went on. 'One day you'll go too far, Sandra, I'm warning you, and then our marriage will really be on the rocks. Be warned.'

His sharply spoken words had more effect on her than any knuckle-rapping would have had, more than his gripping of her hand had had. Silenced, she tripped along behind him. He had never spoken to her like that in all the months she had lived with him. If she had been bad-tempered or irritating he had always laughed at her or coaxed her out of her ill-humour in some way. Never had he reprimanded her as if she were some subordinate of his whom he had discovered making mistakes or doing sloppy work. After a while he said, 'As soon as Liza and Ian arrived yesterday they asked me where you were.'

'Liza said you told them I'd been visiting relatives in England all summer.'

'That's right.'

'Liar. Why lie to them? Why not admit that we've been separated for more than six months?'

'Why should I? The separation, as you call it, has been none of my making. I've asked you twice to come back, using those open, honest methods of which you think so highly, and you've ignored those requests. You wouldn't even stay in London to see me when I called on you. You're so lacking in straightforwardness yourself it seems to me you ask to be tricked and lied to. You behave like an irresponsible juvenile.'

'So it's irresponsible and juvenile for a woman to resent her husband's deliberate deception of her? Well, I don't think so,' she gasped. 'Supposing you had found out I had married you for your wealth and connections . . .'

'Didn't you?' he interrupted drily. 'Didn't Claire put you up to it? Didn't she suggest to you that you follow her example and marry a wealthy man?'

'No, never!' She was aghast. 'Oh, surely you've never thought that I would do something like that?'

'The suspicion has passed through my mind occasionally,' he remarked. 'It's something some women make a career of, marrying a wealthy man and then sueing him for divorce and claiming a large settlement.'

'Cynic,' she accused shakily, appalled that he should have such an opinion of her.

'Cynicism is a by-product of the line of work I'm in,' he retorted. 'Being married to you has increased mine.'

Again she was silenced by his remarks. Conflicting emotions were swirling within her, aroused by the knowldge that he could be as disillusioned by her behaviour as she had been by his. It was something that had never occurred to her before, and now she realised that she had been seeing the situation only from her own point of view, never from his.

'Are the Morisons staying in Venice long?' she asked.

'At least until tomorrow. Ian is now chairman of the

company and he wants to tour the manufacturing companies we own in Italy, meet the managers and some of the personnel.'

'But . . . but . . .' It seemed to Sandra that the whole world was turning upside down. Everything she had known and believed to be stable had altered while she had been in England. 'Claire is chairman . . . I mean chairperson,' she croaked.

'Not any more.'

'Why not?'

'Early in the summer she came to me and told me she didn't want to be chairman any more and asked me what she should do to get out of the company. The problem was trying to find someone already associated with Fontelli's to buy her shares. Eventually I persuaded my uncle to buy some of them. I bought the rest. There was a meeting of the board of directors and Ian was chosen to be chairman for the next five years. Didn't Claire tell you she had resigned when you spoke to her on the phone?'

'No. She was very evasive. She wouldn't even tell me where she is and she didn't want me to go and see her. Do you know her address or where she is staying?'

'I only know the telephone number. I think she's somewhere near Genoa right now but I don't know how long she'll be there.'

'I wish I knew why she decided she wanted out,' Sandra muttered. 'Do you know?'

'Yes, I know. But it's too complicated to explain now. Later, I'll tell you later.'

Later, later, later. He kept saying that. Later he would explain about Claire. Later he would make love to her again. But she wanted to know *now* about Claire, about everything. She was tired of evasions.

'Why won't you tell me now,' she asked.

'Because it would take too long and we're nearly at Mario's,' he replied blandly. 'Anyway, I really think it best if Claire tells you herself. It was her decision.'

'So much seems to have happened while I've been away. So much has changed,' she complained.

'You didn't really think we were all turned into stone when you left, did you?' he jeered. 'Life went on.'

They had reached another junction with a wide street that came across the canal from the left, over another humped-back bridge. There were lights and people. Marco stopped and waited for Liza and Ian to catch up, and then the four of them walked on together, turning right along the wider street. There was no more opportunity for private conversation.

The street spread into a small *piazza* around which narrow apartment houses clustered. A few plane trees with crinkled brown leaves still clinging to their branches cast shadows across the square. From a plain-fronted building next to a bulky baroque church, lights blazed out through latticed windows set under delicate, curved Byzantine arches decorated with lacy stonework. It was Mario's restaurant.

Inside the building was warmth and light. Mario was in the foyer. Short and grey-haired, his broad, black-browed face beamed bright with its wide, white-toothed smile as he bowed over Sandra's hand and kissed it.

'Welcome back, Signora Morosini,' he greeted her in thickly accented English. 'We have missed you so much this past summer.'

'Thank you,' Sandra murmured, surprised that she had been missed. 'You're very kind.'

'I'll take your coat, *signora*,' said Arturo, Mario's doorman, as Mario moved past Sandra exclaiming delightedly in Italian when he saw Liza Morison.

Sandra went up the red-carpeted staircase with Marco. They were going to dine in comparative privacy, he told her, in the long alcove off the dining-room. In the big high-ceilinged room which was decorated with a rich red and gold wallpaper, several people were already seated at round tables, drinking wine while they waited for their food to be prepared. On a raised dais a young man with longish black curly hair was playing a grand piano. As Sandra and Marco passed him on their way to the alcove he looked up. The music came to an abrupt stop and he sprang to his feet, a smile lighting up his thin face.

'Sandra. Is it really you?' he exclaimed, stepping down from the dais. Slightly built, wearing a black tuxedo, dress shirt and black bow-tie, he wasn't much taller than she was. He seized her right hand and raised it to his lips while his big brown eyes expressed their blatant admiration of her. 'It is so good to see you again. Where did you go? And why did you stay away so long? I have missed you.'

Another shock, this time an embarrassing one. She hadn't expected to find Giulio Bertinelli in the restaurant playing the piano. A student of music, whom she had first met during her first few days in Venice, he and his sister had been friendly with her, a friendship that had continued intermittently after her marriage to Marco. Yet she had never until now had to introduce Marco to Giulio.

'How are you?' she asked, withdrawing her hand from his. He seemed to want to hold it for ever. 'I don't think you've ever met Giulio, Marco. He and his sister were very kind to me when I first came to Venice.'

The two men shook hands and murmured to each other in Italian politely but stiffly, and then the awkward moment was over and she and Marco were moving on, past the potted plants that screened the alcove from the main part of the dining-room and Giulio was returning to the piano.

'And why have you never told *me* about *him*?' Silky-smooth, Marco's voice mocked her own much more sharply spoken question about his own failure to tell her about his mother or Ian. 'You should have told me when we got married,' he added accusingly, although still mocking her.

There was no time to answer him, nor did she have an answer ready. The people who were already in the alcove, standing about drinking wine and talking, were turning and coming forward to greet her and Marco.

'You are glad to be back, eh, Sandra?' said Alfredo Gerlini. The lawyer of the Fontelli company who had always been a most supportive friend of Claire's, he was a handsome, silver-haired man of about fifty-five, and he sat at Sandra's left at the elegant oval table while Marco sat to her right. 'There's nowhere else in the world like Venice, and I'm glad to see you here again, with Marco.' He leaned towards her, lowering his voice. 'There has been gossip, you know, that you'd left him, were separated from him. But I hope that is all behind you and you've come back to stay.'

Sandra glanced round the table, wondering how to answer him. Two other company directors and their wives were present besides Alfredo and his wife, and also two close friends of Marco, Toni Manzini, the racing-car driver with his latest girlfriend, and Bernardo Paroni, the well-known Olympic skier. The party was complete, it seemed.

'I haven't come back to be with Marco,' she whispered to Alfredo. 'I've really come to visit Claire.

Marco phoned me last night to tell me she has been in a car accident. But she isn't here and now I've just found out she isn't chairman of the company any more. Do you know where she is, Alfredo?'

'Marco hasn't told you where she's gone?' Alfredo seemed surprised. 'At least, hasn't he told you where she was going when the accident happened?'

'No. He says he has a phone number, that is all, and she must be somewhere near Genoa.'

'Portofino,' said Alfredo, with conviction. 'She was going to Portofino.'

'Thank you. Thank you for telling me,' said Sandra, smiling at him. 'Marco said she left the keys of the apartment with you. I was wondering if I could borrow them from you. You see, I left some of my things there last April . . .'

'Ah, but I don't have the keys any more.' Alfredo's eyes crinkled at the corners as he smiled back at her. 'Liza and her husband, our new chairman, have them. They are living in the apartment now. Francesco arranged it that way, you know, before he died. It is to be used by whoever is chairman of the company. A great man, Francesco. He had wonderful foresight. So all you have to do is ask Liza if you can look for your things. But I'm surprised Claire didn't give your things to Marco when she left.'

'Perhaps she did,' said Sandra hastily, not wanting to be found out in one of her few small lies. She had asked for the keys of the other apartment thinking she could stay the night in it instead of in Marco's apartment, to show him she could be independent of him and that as far as she was concerned they were still separated. 'There hasn't been much time. I only arrived this afternoon,' she added quickly in answer to Alfredo's quizzical glance. 'Late this afternoon. And

. . . well, Marco and I have had much to talk about.' Her cheeks were suddenly on fire as a memory of what she and Marco had done since she had returned stormed into her mind.

'But, of course. You have had much catching up to do after so long a separation,' murmured Alfredo, his eyes glinting knowledgeably. 'It is the same for Teresa and I when I've been away for days on business, isn't it, *cara*?' He turned to his wife, speaking to her in Italian because she didn't know much English. Plump and placid-looking, her white throat and fingers ablaze with diamonds, Teresa nodded, her dark eyes also twinkling with a knowledgeable gleam as she smiled at Sandra.

While Alfredo continued to talk to his wife Sandra sank back in her chair and sipped some wine. At least she knew where Claire was. Tomorrow she would find a way of travelling to the Italian Riviera. She imagined a map of Italy. All she had to do was get to Milan and then to Genoa. From Genoa it would be easy to travel to Portofino.

'Marco.' She touched his arm and he excused himself to Liza to whom he had been talking and turned his head. His grey eyes softened as they met hers and he touched her fingers which were still resting on his arm. She felt the usual thrill of excitement when he touched her and was immediately angry with herself for being so vulnerable, reminding herself that he was probably only touching her hand for the benefit of anyone who might be watching them, wanting his friends and colleagues to believe that he and she were reconciled. 'Alfredo has told me that Claire is in Portofino,' she said in firm, cool tones, as she withdrew her hand from his arm. 'I'll leave in the morning and go to see her. I can return to London from Genoa. I have to be back at work on Monday morning.'

He stopped pretending. His eyes grew as cold and clear as icicles and his lips tightened.

'We'll talk about it later,' he said. Reaching out he lifted the leather-covered, gold-embossed menu from the table and turned to her again. 'Have you decided what you would like to eat? You must be hungry. I don't suppose you've eaten since lunch on the plane.'

He was opening the menu, putting on an act of being attentive to her, of caring about her, when someone came behind them, actually leaned between them, and a woman's voice with a hint of laughter in it said, 'Marco, *caro mio*. Here I am. So sorry to be late. The plane was a long time landing. And Sandra. So pleased to see you here. I had heard . . . but no matter what I heard . . . it is good to see you.'

Dark, almost frizzy hair swinging forward along a slim, tanned cheek. Thin red lips curving back over almond-shaped teeth. Black eyes sparkling like jet. Long punky earrings glittering and dangling almost to the shoulders. Lucia Spenola, lean and tall, dynamic in a purple and red woollen dress, the high collar clipped with a diamanté brooch and waist belted with red suede. Lucia was actually there, between them, kissing Marco on the cheek and then after the slightest of hesitations kissing Sandra too!

Sandra was so amazed that she missed entirely hearing Marco's reply to Lucia. All she could think of was that this woman she hated so much was there, had been expected at the dinner. Otherwise, why would Lucia be apologising for being late? Lucia had been expected and that meant she had been invited. By whom? By Marco, of course. He had arranged the dinner.

'But I was hoping I could sit near you and Sandra.' Lucia's high voice with its nasal New York drawl, complaining, sliced through the haze of bewilderment and fury that was clouding Sandra's mind. The haze cleared and she realised that changes were being made at the table to accommodate Lucia. Toni and his girlfriend were moving around, away from Bernardo, and a chair was being placed in the space they had made, 'I have so much to tell you, Marco,' Lucia went on.

'It'll wait,' said Marco, at his suavest. 'Come on, I'll show you to your seat.'

He pushed back his chair, smiled briefly at Sandra and excused himself. She sat stiffly, unable to return his smile. How could he do this to her? she thought, watching him walk with Lucia around the table, stopping here and there to talk to the others. How could he have brought her to this dinner knowing that Lucia might come in? How could he have arranged for her to meet Lucia again in front of all these people, all of whom probably knew about his affair with Lucia and were watching now for some reaction from herself.

Well, they were not going to be disappointed, she fumed inwardly. She wasn't one of those passive wives. She wasn't like Teresa Gerlini. She wasn't going to stay and be humiliated further by the presence of her husband's mistress at the same table as herself. She was leaving.

She was on her feet almost before she knew it, excusing herself to Liza and then to Alfredo, backing away from her place and turning to the archway. She had gone only a few steps when someone stepped in front of her. She stopped, her gaze travelling upwards over fine grey suiting with a thin red line, over a sparkling white shirt collar, a square chin with an attractive cleft in it, over generously curved yet firm lips right up to ice-cold eyes.

'Where are you going?' Marco demanded softly.

'To ... to the ladies room. I won't be long,' she whispered.

'You'd better not be,' he said, eyes narrowing menacingly and she could see he was speaking through gritted teeth. 'I'll come in there to get you if you're more than ten minutes!'

He stepped sideways and she passed him, going through the archway and down the two shallow steps and into the dining-room, walking sedately while she suppressed an urge to take to her heels and scurry amongst the tables to the stairs. At last she reached the staircase and began to run down. The music Giulio was playing seemd to float mockingly after her. It was the ballad from an old film about World War Two, 'Casablanca', and it was suggesting to her that she remember a kiss is still a kiss, a sigh is still a sigh. Completely romantic and sentimental, it derided what she was doing or planning to do, almost persuading her not to run away from Marco for a second time but to accept his kisses and love-making at face value and forget his association with Lucia; to take what he offered and be satisfied.

The song came to an end as she reached the foyer. She had about eight minutes left of the ten Marco had dictated she could have before he came looking for her. Arturo was in the foyer and when she asked him for her coat he brought it immediately, without question, trained as he was to serve people to the best of his ability. He was helping her on with the coat when Giulio came down the stairs. Giulio was not so un-inquisitive.

'Sandra, where are you going? Why are you leaving so early? You can't have had anything to eat yet,' he exclaimed coming right over to her. Velvety dark, his big brown eyes regarded her anxiously. 'I hope nothing unusual has happened to call you away from the party.'

'I can't stay,' she muttered. 'I have to leave. Why aren't you still playing the piano?' With swift fingers she fastened her raincoat, tied the belt and pulled the hood up over her head.

'It's my break,' he said, placing a cigarette in his mouth. 'You like the way I play?'

'Yes, of course I do. Thank you, Arturo.' She placed a tip in the doorman's hand as he swung the door open for her. 'Would you like to walk a little way across the *piazza* with me?' she asked Giulio.

'It will be a pleasure,' he replied.

As soon as they were outside and the door had closed after them Sandra took hold of Giulio's arm, urging him across the square with her.

'I have to hurry,' she explained. 'I'd like to get to the landing stage at the Rialto Bridge by the shortest possible route. I must catch a waterbus. I want to get to Mestre tonight.'

'Then come this way,' said Giulio obligingly and together they began to walk in the direction of a street that angled away from the square.

'I cannot help being curious,' Giulio said as they stepped from the square into a narrow, winding lane edged by small shops which were now closed for the night. 'But why are you leaving alone? Where are you going by yourself?'

'I'm going to see Claire Fontelli. She's at Portofino,

near Genoa and I've decided that if I could stay the
night in Mestre I'd be able to catch an early bus for
Milan in the morning.'

'But ... forgive me for not understanding,' said
Giulio in his gentle way, 'why can't your husband take
you to Portofino? In the car he drives you could be
there easily by tomorrow afternoon.'

'He hasn't time to drive me there. I have to go by
myself. Do you know of a good hotel where I could
stay the night in Mestre?'

'I do. But I know of somewhere better than a hotel.
Angela, my sister, has an apartment over there. You
could stay the night with her.'

'Could I really?' Sandra felt a sudden warm rush of
affection for him. 'Oh, I'm glad I asked you. Will it be
hard to find where she lives?' To herself, she was
thinking Marco would never find her if she stayed
with Angela, whereas he might try every hotel in
Mestre once he had realised she had left him again.

'This is her address.' Giulio told her the name of the
street and the number of the block of apartments.
'Angela is in 501 and when I get back to Mario's I'll
phone her and tell her to expect you.'

They had reached the end of the street and there
were the dark waters of a narrow canal shimmering
with reflected lights. A gondola poled by silently.

'Cross the bridge and you'll find yourself in Calle
Merceria. You know the way from there,' said Giulio.
'But before you go, Sandra, tell me why you're leaving
your husband again. Isn't he kind to you?'

She turned to him in surprise. She hadn't realised he
knew she had left Marco once. In the glow of a street
lamp his dark eyes looked at her curiously and with
some puzzlement.

'I can't stay with him knowing that he is deceiving

me all the time,' she whispered. 'Some women don't mind if . . . if their husband has a mistress. In this country and others it has been an accepted way of life. But I can't . . . I can't live with or be dependent on a man whom I know spends part of his time with another woman.'

'Don't you love him any more?' asked Giulio, still looking puzzled.

'I don't know. I'm not sure. All I know is that I daren't stay the night here in Venice with him. I have to get away now.' She paused, biting her lip, suddenly not as trusting of him any more. He was, after all, a man, and might take Marco's side. 'You won't tell him I'm going to stay with Angela, will you, Giulio? He might ask you if you've seen me when you get back to Mario's. Please don't tell him. I don't want him to know.'

'I shall be careful to avoid him,' he replied reassuringly.

'Thank you. Goodnight. I shan't forget you or your friendship.'

She hurried along the winding street. By the time she reached the landing stage by the pale Rialto Bridge she was breathless and her head was swimming with a weakness she knew was due to hunger. A *vaporetto* was just ready to depart for the station and she ran on to it, guessing that if she didn't catch it there would be a long wait at that time of night for the next, and during that time Marco might guess where she had gone and come after her. He was too clever and cunning not to have guessed she would make for the landing stage and the one way by which she could leave Venice.

Thank God she had all her money, her passport and her credit cards in her handbag with her, she thought

as she sat down. Thank God, too, that Giulio had been
taking his break as she had left Mario's. She smiled a
little as she stared out at the dim palaces sliding by,
thinking of the fun she had once experienced with
Giulio and his sister, going with them to concerts and
dancing at discothèques. That had been before Marco
had started to take an interest in her, before he had
taken her over, whisking her off to the Lido, or driving
her up into the mountains.

Oh, why had she ever let him bewitch her into
marrying him? Why couldn't she have fallen in love
with someone her own age; someone like Giulio?
Someone honest and open-handed? She was no match
either for Marco the sophisticated financial wizard or
for Marco the lover of pleasure, the hedonist who
thought nothing of dining with his wife and mistress at
the same time. At the memory of Lucia's sudden
appearance at Mario's that night, like the appearance
of a wicked fairy in some fairy tale, Sandra ground her
teeth and clenched her hands. Never, never would she
understand Marco, how he could make love to her as
he had done that evening and then greet Lucia, the
other woman in his life, so easily without any
embarrassment.

The *vaporetto* lurched against the landing stage near
the Piazzale Roma and she disembarked with the few
other passengers. It didn't take long for her to find a
taxi, and soon she was travelling across the Ponte della
Libertà, towards the dark spaces of industry looming
against the illuminated sky, towards Mestre and
Marghera where Francesco Fontelli and other
progressive Venetians of his time had founded their
factories and businesses to make the money necessary
to keep Venice alive. Beauty, it seemed, could not

survive without the support of polluting commercial developments.

The taxi driver knew where Angela lived, and within an hour of leaving Mario's Sandra was ascending in a lift to the fifth floor of a plain brick building of small apartments. The door of 501 was flung open by an excited Angela, a smaller, rounder edition of Giulio. She embraced Sandra affectionately and pulled her into the living-room of the small flat.

'I couldn't believe it when Giulio told me you were coming,' Angela exclaimed. She spoke English slowly, dropping 'h's, hardening the 'th' to 'd' and lengthening all the vowels. 'But he is a little worried about you.'

'Why?' Sandra sank down thankfully on to a settee from which the untidy, artistic Angela had swept books and sketches to the floor.

'I think he is afraid of your husband. Marco is much bigger and stronger than Giulio. Also he has much influence in Venice because he is wealthy. Giulio says that if Marco asks him if he knows where you are he is afraid he will not be able to lie to him,' said Angela. 'Giulio is afraid Marco might threaten him.'

'Well, we'll just have to hope Marco doesn't ask Giulio,' sighed Sandra. 'I'm so hungry, Angela, I can't really get worried about them. Do you think I could have something to eat, please? I left before I had time to even choose my dinner.'

'I will get you something right now. And while we eat, we'll talk. But first you must tell me why you're running away from Marco again. Is he so cruel? Does he beat you?'

'Oh, no. Nothing like that. He just deceived me all the time,' replied Sandra wearily.

'I see,' said Angela frowning in the same way that

Giulio had, looking puzzled which meant she didn't 'see' at all.

Angela made some open sandwiches of fresh Italian bread and chicken pâté, and while she wolfed down the food Sandra told her friend why she had left Marco in April, how he had tricked her into returning to Venice and then had humiliated her by inviting Lucia to be present at the dinner party at Mario's. There was some relief in confiding in the dreamy-eyed Italian woman, but as she talked Sandra began to see a new version of herself. Her own behaviour seemed to have been that of an over-sensitive adolescent completely lacking in self-confidence and not that of the independent, mature woman she had believed herself to be. The discovery that possibly she hadn't grown up emotionally yet, was another shock to add to all the others she had received that day.

'I know of Marco, of course,' said Angela slowly. 'I have seen him dashing about in his speedboat. He is handsome and rich and I would think he is a good lover, strong yet gentle.' She rolled her eyes and made a gesture with one hand that meant she approved of men who were good lovers.

'Being a good lover is not the only recommendation a man requires to be a good husband,' argued Sandra.

'But it is a very important one,' said Angela. 'And if Marco were my husband I wouldn't run away from him. I would stick to him, never let him out of my sight, never give another woman a chance to get him.' She studied Sandra seriously. 'But perhaps you do not love him, not properly, not enough.'

'The point is, he doesn't love me,' retorted Sandra. 'He wouldn't have invited Lucia to the dinner tonight if he loved me properly and enough.'

'Doesn't he make love to you any more?' asked

Angela curiously.

Once again Sandra found her cheeks burning as memories of Marco's lovemaking that evening flooded her mind. Marco's hands caressing her body, his lips stroking her skin, his voice whispering to her as the black magic of his lovemaking had spun her round and round. It was impossible for her to continue to face Angela's curious glance. Her eyelids drooped.

'Aha, you give yourself away,' mocked Angela. 'Marco makes love to you so that means he wants you, and while he wants you there is always the chance he is still in love with you or will fall in love with you again.'

'We'll never agree on this,' sighed Sandra. 'Our attitudes to love are so different. For you, for Marco, probably for Giulio, love is mostly physical.'

'But not for you?' Angela looked astonished. 'You are cold then, as I have read that English women often are? What is the word? Frigid? Ah, Sandra *mia*, how terrible for you. Think of what you must be missing. Can't anything be done . . .'

'No, no.' Sandra found quite surprisingly she was laughing. Talking to Angela was much more comforting than talking to Thea was. Thea was so tense, so serious, so anti-male. Angela, on the other hand, loved the opposite sex and lived for love. 'I'm not frigid. At least I don't think so. I'm just not convinced that *making* love is all there is to loving a person. There has to be more, a meeting of minds, a sharing of feelings and thoughts.'

'But that will come,' said Angela. 'After you have been married for a while. You have been married for how long? Not much more than a year? And you expect perfection already? I find you very funny. How can you share anything with Marco or get to know him better if you continue to run away from him? I think you should go back to him tomorrow and forget about going to Portofino.'

'No, I couldn't do that,' said Sandra stubbornly. 'Not now.'

'You mean you are too proud to go back and apologise and admit you have made a mistake?' suggested Angela. 'Then it would seem you don't love him any more. And you have never given him the chance to explain. You assume arrogantly that you are in the right all the time and he is in the wrong. Yet he has shown he is willing to meet you half-way. He asked you to come back to Venice . . .'

'He tricked me into coming,' insisted Sandra.

'So what is wrong in that? He must have wanted you back very badly to trick you. Can't you see that?'

'No, I can't. He wanted me to be at that dinner party so that everyone there would believe he and I had become reconciled.'

'Everyone? Even Lucia?' queried Angela.

Sandra bit her lip. It hadn't occurred to her that Marco might have also wanted to convince Lucia that his marriage was still 'on' so to speak.

Angela stood up.

'You're tired,' she murmured. 'You can't think straight any more. And no wonder. Too much has happened today. I'll show you where the bedroom is. You can have the bed. I'll sleep in here on the settee.'

'Do you know what time the bus leaves for Milan in the morning,' asked Sandra, stifling a yawn.

'You can catch one at the end of this street at nine-thirty.'

'Will you wake me in time to catch it? I'm afraid I might oversleep, I'm so tired.'

'I'll do that,' Angela promised.

The narrow bed in the small cupboard of a room

was hard, but Sandra hardly noticed. Although no one had attacked her with violence, she felt beaten and bruised mentally by all the shocks and surprises she had experienced since Marco had phoned her the previous night. No sooner had she settled her head on the pillow than she fell asleep, a merciful blanket blotting out the confusion that raged in her mind.

CHAPTER FIVE

SHE was in a huge ballroom. Brilliant crystal chandeliers glittered overhead. She was waltzing, turning round and round, and the skirt of her long satin dress was whirling out. Her partner was Kevin Collins, with whom she worked at the library in London. He was in the full dress uniform of some Guards regiment. Suddenly, someone pushed between them, a tall, dark-haired man dressed in grey. He seized her hand and began to drag her across the room. Her hand was hurting and she was gasping for breath. Trying to twist her hand free, she shouted out, 'No, Marco, no!'

'Sandra, Sandra, wake up.' A gentle, familiar female voice with an Italian accent spoke to her and she opened her eyes, the bright sunlight slanting in through a small curtained window. She looked up at the serenely smiling face of Angela who, dressed in a silky dressing-gown, was standing beside the narrow bed with a mug in her hand.

'I've brought you some coffee to wake you up,' Angela said. 'He is here, your husband, Marco. He has come for you.'

'What?' Sandra sat up abruptly, the dream fading from her mind. Her left hand had no feeling in it and she guessed she must have either been lying on it or had had it higher than her head as she slept, so that the blood had drained out of it. She rubbed it vigorously. 'What do you mean, Marco is here? If it's your idea of a joke, Angela . . .'

'No, no.' Angela shook her head, her brown eyes

very serious as she handed over the mug of coffee. 'It is true. He is here. In the other room drinking coffee, too. Shall I tell him to come to you, to come in here?'

'Oh. No, don't do that. I . . . I'll get up and get dressed,' gasped Sandra. 'But how did he know I'd be here?' She took a gulp of strong black coffee, then all that had happened the previous evening came rushing into her mind and she groaned. 'Giulio must have told him. Marco must have threatened Giulio in some way, forced him to tell. Angela have you heard from Giulio? Is he all right?'

'I haven't heard from Giulio and I'm sure he's all right,' replied Angela. 'Marco will tell you how he found out you were here.' She frowned a little, seemed about to say something, then changed her mind and muttered, 'I'll leave you to get dressed.'

She left the room and Sandra drained the coffee-mug, set it down and got out of bed. Fortunately the bathroom could be reached through a door from the bedroom and she was able to go to it without passing through the living-room and encountering Marco.

Her first reaction, after worrying about Giulio, to the news that Marco had come after her was one of strange triumph and pleasure. He had found out where she had gone and come after her. Didn't that mean he still wanted her in spite of her behaviour last night? Even though she had let him down, had walked out on the dinner party he had arranged to celebrate her return to Venice, he still cared sufficiently to follow her, to make her go back with him, perhaps. She thought of how angry he must have been, might still be, because she had left the restaurant without telling him, because she had embarrassed him in front of his friends and relatives, and she felt a shiver of fear. Facing him again in Angela's tiny living-room with Angela looking on wasn't going to be easy.

Yet when she entered the living-room, having dressed in the only clothes she had with her—the emerald-green gown she had worn for dining out—Marco was sitting at his ease on the settee and talking amicably to Angela who, seated on a leather-covered ottoman, was gazing at him with an expression that Sandra could only describe as rapturous. Once more, she thought, with a touch of wry humour, Marco, like Julius Caesar, had come, had seen and had conquered.

Uncertainly, she stood in the dorway looking at him. This morning he was more like the Marco she had first met and with whom she had fallen in love. Black hair, slightly ruffled, profile severely aloof, a white, high-necked sweater accentuating the olive tint of his skin, a black and red quilted ski-jacket unzipped over his sweater, well-cut black trousers, elegant black suede shoes. Black and red. The colours of the Fontelli coat of arms. Why had she never noticed before how often Marco wore those two colours? He saw her and rose to his feet, walked across to her.

'Good morning, *cara mia*,' he said softly and bending his head kissed her lightly on the lips. 'I hope you have slept well.'

'Good morning,' she whispered.

How calm he was. How completely in control of the situation. And yet she found his suave, polite behaviour more disturbing than any show of anger would have been. It made her wonder what trick he had up his sleeve this time. How was he going to deceive her today? The grey eyes smiled down into hers, yet there was no warmth in them. They were cold, calculating, watching alertly for her next move. Sandra gave herself a little mental shake. No need to show how afraid she was of him.

'I'm surprised to see you here,' she said, tilting her chin, looking him straight in the eyes. 'How did you know where to find me?'

'Someone with your interests at heart informed me,' he replied coolly and evasively. 'Have you forgotten, *cara mia*, that I promised yesterday I would take you to see Claire? I have come this morning to carry out my promise to drive you to Portofino.'

'Oh, but . . .' She felt trapped and glanced rather wildly at Angela who nodded at her encouragingly. 'You don't have to drive me. I can go by bus. I have it all planned. I'm going to catch the bus at the end of this street at nine-thirty.'

He raised one dark eyebrow. His lips curved in a slight but mocking smile. He glanced at the watch on his wrist.

'You have missed that bus,' he said. 'It's now five to ten, so you'd best take up my offer to drive you to Portofino.'

Sandra looked at Angela reproachfully.

'You didn't wake me up in time,' she said.

'I thought it would be better if you slept longer,' replied Angela, not in the least disconcerted.

'Coming with me will allow you to keep *your* promise to me,' Marco pointed out and she looked back at him.

'What promise?'

'You agreed to discuss the situation between us now that you're here.' He stepped close to her and she seemed to be enveloped suddenly in the cloak of his personal magnetism. The warmth of him, the scents of his skin, seemed to reach out and draw her close to him even though he didn't touch her. Flaring smokily, his eyes looked right into hers and she felt her knees shake. But when he spoke, although his voice was soft, there was a cutting edge beneath the surface smoothness. 'You didn't really believe I'd let you go so easily, did you, *cara mia*?'

She looked away quickly to Angela again, but surprisingly her friend had left the room. Biting a corner of her lower lip, still keeping her gaze averted from Marco, she muttered, 'But don't you have work to do? It will take most of today to drive to Portofino. I wouldn't want to take you away from your work.'

'I'm not tied to time. We will have a few hours together, alone,' he pointed out calmly. 'I'd have preferred to have spent the time with you at the apartment or walking round Venice, but I promised I would take you to see Claire and she is now expecting you. I phoned her to tell her you would be arriving about sunset today.'

'And she didn't object?' She glanced in surprise at him.

'No.' His lips curved in a cynical grin. 'She knows better than to object to anything I say I'm going to do,' he drawled. 'She has more sense than you have.' The grin faded. 'So, are you ready to leave now?' he asked. 'I have your case in the car. Travelling with me will be much faster and more comfortable than going by bus and having to change at Milan and Genoa.'

'How do I know you'll drive me to Portofino? How do I know this isn't another of your deceitful tricks?' she demanded.

'You'll just have to trust me. I only resort to tricks when other, more straightforward methods fail,' he replied coldly. Then suddenly his eyes flashed her a bright, shrivelling glance and he leaned closer to her, almost threateningly. 'After the way you behaved last night you're damned lucky I'm here at all,' he said roughly. 'Last night I was in a mood to commit murder when I found you'd left Mario's, so thank your lucky stars I didn't find you then. I didn't find out where you'd gone until this morning.' A movement in the doorway drew their attention and he stepped back from her. 'So where is your coat?' he asked, pleasantly polite once more.

Angela had returned and was lingering by the door. Her brown eyes gazed intently at Sandra as if she were trying to convey a message. Remembering that Angela had accused her, admittedly very gently, of having been arrogant in not allowing Marco to explain about his association with Lucia, Sandra suddenly lowered the barrier of her pride. Turning back to Marco she said, 'My coat is in the bedroom.' She held her head high. She wasn't giving in to him or letting him take over, she argued with herself. She was merely going to be fair and allow him a chance to explain.

'I'll get it,' said Angela brightly, as if keen for Sandra to leave with Marco. She was back within seconds, the raincoat over one arm.

'Perhaps we could have breakfast on the way,' Sandra said as she slipped her arms into the sleeves of the raincoat.

'Of course,' Marco murmured. He was already on his way to the door of the flat.

'*Buon giorno, signorina,*' he said pleasantly to Angela, smiling at her. 'And thank you for your help.'

'Goodbye, Angie.' Sandra kissed her friend and whispered, 'Thanks for letting me stay here and say goodbye to Giulio for me.'

'I have something to confess to you,' whispered Angela, putting her arms around Sandra and holding her close. 'This morning, Giulio and I decided Marco must be told you were here. I phoned Marco early, told him you were here with me and he asked me to keep you here until he arrived. That is why I let you oversleep. It was for the best, Sandra. He has a right to know where you are. He's your husband. Forgive us, Giulio and me?'

'I suppose so,' sighed Sandra.

'You'll be back soon, in Venice. I know it,' said Angela. 'You belong here with *him. Arrivederci.*'

It wasn't until they were on the highway to Milan that Marco broke the silence between them. He went straight to the point.

'Why did you leave Mario's last night with the piano player? Was a stroll in the moonlight with him more important than dining with me and helping to entertain my guests?'

'Giulio only showed me how to get to the Rialto. He went back to Mario's,' she replied calmly.

'Don't lie to me,' he retorted viciously.

'I'm not lying,' she protested hotly. 'After he'd shown me the way he went back to Mario's. You must know he did. You must have seen him and heard him playing the piano.'

'He didn't return to Mario's. In fact Mario was more than a little mad because Giulio didn't return.'

'Then where did he go?' she exclaimed.

'To Mestre with you. To his sister's apartment, to spend the night with you,' he accused between set teeth.

She spent the next few minutes struggling to cope with this new shock. Speech seemed to have deserted her. She could only stare at his darkly etched classical profile.

'Couldn't you have waited until the dinner party was over before going with him?' Marco enquired coldly when she didn't speak.

'I didn't go with him to Mestre. He wasn't at

Angela's apartment and I didn't spend the night with him. He ... he must have been too afraid of you to return to Mario's, afraid you'd threaten him if he didn't tell you where I'd gone,' she whispered.

'Then why did you leave if it wasn't to go with him?'

He couldn't look at her. He was too busy driving, overtaking container lorries and other vehicles that were moving along in the slow lane. But she could sense the anger boiling in him and she was afraid of it. She was afraid it might affect his driving and make him take risks; afraid he might drive them both to their deaths, there on the highway. She had never known him to be angry like this before.

'Can't you guess why I left?' she asked.

'I have guessed, but you say I'm mistaken. If you didn't leave because you preferred to be with Giulio why did you leave?' To her relief, he seemed to be simmering down and was speaking more reasonably.

'Didn't you follow me as soon as you found out I'd left with Giulio?'

'How could I? I had guests to think of. I couldn't rush out straight away. I had to go back to them, apologise on your behalf.'

'What did you tell them?'

'That you didn't feel well and that I was taking you back to the apartment.'

'You lied, you pretended,' she accused.

'I did what was necessary,' he retorted coldly.

'Did you go the apartment?'

'No. I walked around the square for a while then I walked back to the restaurant.'

'To be with Lucia, I suppose,' she sniped.

'To be with my guests,' he shot back at her. He slowed down the car and steered it into an exit road for the city of Padua. 'We'll stop here for breakfast. It's a good place.'

He drove into a wayside service centre where there was a restaurant and gift shop as well as petrol and diesel oil pumps. Marco parked the car amongst others, turned off the engine and looked at her.

'Are you going to give me a reason for leaving the dinner party last night without apology or explanation? Or do I have to continue to believe you went off with Giulio to spend the night with him?' he demanded, his eyes narrow and hostile, his mouth stern.

'I couldn't stay while Lucia was there,' she answered. 'How you had the nerve to invite her, I'll never understand. I had to leave. I couldn't stay in the same room as her.'

'Then why the hell didn't you say so when I asked you where you were going?'

'I . . . I was too upset,' she replied, trying to remember how she had felt. 'I had to get away from all of you. You were all watching me to see how I would behave with her there. To see if I would turn a blind eye to the presence of my husband's mistress . . .'

'Lucia is not my mistress,' he hissed at her and opening the door beside him he got out. He slammed the door shut and walked away towards the restaurant. He didn't seem to care if she followed him or not and he hadn't shown his usual courtesy and come round to her side of the car to open the door for her. He was obviously too angry to be polite.

She wished she didn't have to follow him into the restautant. She wished she could run away again, from his scornful anger this time, but she was hungry again and there were still explanations to be made and heard. She could almost feel Angela at her side urging her to give Marco a chance to explain.

The restaurant was the self-service kind and full of lorry drivers. Hearing the mixture of languages being spoken, Sandra felt as if she had stepped into a meeting of the European Economic Community. Marco was already serving himself with food so she went to the end of the queue to take her turn. When her tray was full and she had paid she joined him at a table for two by a window. Sunlight slanted in. The room was warm and noisy. She took off her raincoat and sat down.

He had bought a newspaper, had folded it beside his tray and was reading it. Not for the first time since she had first met him she thought of how remote he could be. He seemed to be able to cut himself off from his immediate surroundings and the people he was with. He was unapproachable, and she wished suddenly and heartily he could be as easily approached as Giulio or even Kevin Collins.

But, then, if he were like Giulio or Kevin she would never have fallen in love with him, was her next irrepressible thought. It was his cool aloofness that made him so attractive to her; in the way that a high mountain peak, often hidden by clouds, attracts a climber. When she was with him he fascinated her, she realised, and she wanted to reach out to him, draw his attention to her somehow, possibly by irresponsible wayward behaviour, by any means she could find.

For a while they didn't speak, both being busy eating. Not until she finished her omelette did Sandra break the silence.

'Why didn't you say that Lucia isn't your mistress in April, when I asked you?' she said.

'Mmm?' He looked up from reading the newspaper. 'Sorry. What did you say?'

Suppressing an indignant retort she repeated her question. He frowned slightly. 'Did you *ask* me in April if she was?' he retorted coolly. 'My memory of that little scene before you flung out of the apartment and never came back is that you accused me of having had an affair with her when I lived in the States and of never telling you about it. You didn't wait for me to ask you what you were talking about or explain.'

'Well, you didn't deny it,' she said, holding on to her temper with difficulty.

'Didn't deny that I'd had an affair with her, do you mean?' he queried, raising his eyebrows. 'I couldn't because it was true. Lucia and I did date each other when I was at Wharton studying for my MBA. Not exactly what is known as an affair today. We didn't sleep together.' His lips twisted together in a wry grin. 'Lucia's mother made sure of that. Both she and Lucia were aiming for marriage first.'

'Why didn't you marry her?'

'I found out something that made marriage between us out of the question,' he said evasively and shrugged. 'It's time we were on the road again. That is, if you still want to go and see Claire.'

'Yes, I still want to see her. That's why I came, remember, to see her, not you,' she retorted. 'But I'd like to clear up this matter of Lucia before we start driving again. Why did she imply that she was your mistress when I met her in April? She told me that you and she had always been very close and that you stayed with her every time you visited the States.'

'She did it out of spite.' The cynical curve to his lips was back. 'Some women are like that, you know.'

'And some men are, too.' She was up in arms at once at what she considered to be a sexist remark.

'Granted,' he drawled. 'And I didn't invite Lucia to

that dinner party,' he added, glaring at her across the table. 'So you can stop thinking I invited her to annoy you. When I think of all the trouble I went to to get you there, only to have you run out on me at the last minute just because she turned up, I feel like retreating to a monastery where there wouldn't be any women.' He drew a hissing breath. 'I didn't know Lucia was in Venice or expected to be in Venice until she walked into the dining-room at Mario's. Got that straight?'

She could only nod to show she believed him. Pride wouldn't let her show the dismay she was feeling because once again, thanks to Lucia, she had jumped to a wrong conclusion and had run away.

'But she must have known about the dinner,' she muttered after a few moments of strained silence.

'Liza told her about it. Told her too that you would be there,' he said. 'That's why she came. She knew you would be there, that you had come back.'

'I can't see why she should be spiteful to me,' she murmured. 'I'd never met her, had never heard of her until she turned up in Venice in April.'

'It isn't you who has earned her spite, it's me. She's never forgiven me for not asking her to marry me, so she's determined to wreck my marriage to you.' He paused then added cynically, 'She's nearly succeeded too. And all because you believed her in April. You believed her and didn't trust me. If you'd trusted me in April you wouldn't have left me. If you'd trusted me last night you wouldn't have walked out of that dinner party.'

'But how could I trust you?' she cried out in self-defence, her voice rising and drawing the attention of two lorry drivers at the next table. 'If only you'd told me about Lucia before I ever met her,' she said in a lower voice, leaning towards him across the table. 'If only you'd told me more about yourself, about your family for instance, I'd have been more willing to understand. I wanted to know more about you ...'

'At the time you seemed quite happy to accept me as I was—and as I still am,' he reminded her quietly.

'You didn't accept me as I was and still am without question,' she argued fiercely. 'You knew I was Claire's daughter and you married me because I was related to her, because she owned all those shares.'

'She doesn't own them now,' he was quick to point out. 'Now the shoe is on the other foot and I own the majority of the shares and my uncle is the chairman.' He laughed jeeringly and sank back in his chair, his eyes sparkling with cold derision. 'So if you say that you now want to end our separation and stay married to me I'm going to be pretty suspicious of you, aren't I?'

His mockery struck home sharply, as she was sure it was intended to. He was taking his revenge on her for her lack of trust in him and he was enjoying it. Her two reasons for leaving him in April were no longer valid, so it seemed, if she could believe what he had said about Lucia. And she wanted to believe him. She wanted desperately to believe him.

'Are you going to tell me why Claire sold her shares?' she asked.

'No.'

'Why not?'

'You might not believe me. And it's her business, not mine, why she sold them. Best for her to tell you herself. You're more likely to *believe* her.'

Another dagger thrust. He was good at giving them and there seemed to be no gentleness in him any more. None for her, at least. He was treating her as if she was someone he didn't care for and had never cared for.

'Marco, I'm sorry I ... I ran away last night,' she began slowly. 'I ... I wouldn't have done if Lucia hadn't arrived. Oh, it's so hard to describe to you how I felt. I felt sick ...'

'And that is what I told everyone,' he put in drily. 'You felt sick.'

'Did they believe you?'

'I don't know. I wasn't going to tell them the truth, that you'd walked out, let me down. I wasn't going to give Lucia the satisfaction of guessing she had achieved what she'd set out to do. With a little help from you, she's managed to wreck what you and I had until she came on the scene,' he said coolly. 'Now I've found out that you don't trust me and never have. And I've found out about Giulio.'

'But there's nothing between me and Giulio. Nothing at all. I didn't spend the night with him.' The lorry drivers were looking at her and Marco again, their eyes bright with curiosity. 'Giulio and I aren't lovers. I swear it. We're not, we're not.'

'Swearing isn't much good. Taking an oath these days to tell the truth doesn't hold much water,' he remarked cynically, pushing back his chair and rising to his feet. 'People are taking oaths and then telling lies all the time. You'll have to prove it.'

'I can't. Not here,' she whispered, looking up at him. Never had he looked so hard, so unrelenting to her. 'You'll have to take my word for it. You'll have to,' she insisted, getting quickly to her feet as she realised he was on the move.

'Why should I?' he retorted. 'Really, Sandra, you're something else. You don't trust me. You don't believe anything I say, so why the hell should I take your word for anything?'

His revenge was complete. He had turned the tables

on her, and now she appeared to be the guilty party, or at least he was implying that she was, basing the implication on her behaviour last night when she had left Mario's with Giulio.

Disconsolately she trudged after him across the car park to the Ferrari.

'So what are we going to do now?' she asked hesitantly when the car was on the highway again, roaring past lorries.

'We could get a divorce,' he said. 'It would be the best way out, I think, since you don't seem to want to come to terms with my way of life. You see, I didn't marry you for you to live in London pursuing what you call a career while I live a bachelor existence in Venice. I'm not made that way. I'm not cold-blooded enough. I married you because I wanted a wife who would also be my lover and the mother of my children. I hoped, when I married you, that you would be that sort of wife. It seems you can't be so we'd better cut the bond, quickly and cleanly. What do you think?'

Confusion raged in her mind again. She hadn't expected this from him. She had been going to suggest divorce. But that had been before she had seen him again, before he had made love to her again, before she had realised she had made a mistake by believing Lucia was his mistress.

'I . . . I think that you don't love me,' she murmured. 'Not the me that I am, I mean,' she added quickly, her thoughts muddled as usual. 'You said . . . you said yesterday, last night, that I had lived in a romantic dream in which you starred as the rich prince who had married Cinderella. Well, I think you've been living in a sort of dream too, in which I star as a sort of super woman who can be the perfect hostess for your guests, who never makes mistakes or behaves foolishly. You don't love me. You love an image you have made of the sort of wife you think you ought to have.'

'You're wrong, as usual,' he murmured, with a brief self-mocking laugh. 'I love you, the you that you are. Or I did until last night.' His breath came harshly. 'But last night opened my eyes. I saw for the first time you didn't care enough for me to stay at my side at that dinner party. It was a party to celebrate our getting together again, or so I planned it to be, but you had to show everyone you didn't care by walking out. You don't love me and never have. If you had, you wouldn't have run away last April and you wouldn't have left last night.'

Fields and factories flicked by. Exits to cities and villages loomed up and were passed. The sky clouded over and a fine misty rain slicked the Tarmac and blurred the distant foothills of the Alps. Steadily, swiftly, they were getting nearer to Milan.

Numbed by Marco's cold analysis of the situation between them which demolished completely her own confused argument, Sandra leaned back and closed her eyes. For the moment she could think of nothing to say, no more questions to ask, no more accusations to make. Nothing had worked out as she had expected when she had left London yesterday morning, and now she was wishing she could go back in time. If only she could go back a day to her arrival at Venice airport yesterday. No, if only she could go back to last April, before Lucia had arrived . . .

She could go on for ever, she realised, trying to get back to a period of time when all was well between herself and Marco, when she had been sure of his love and he of hers, when they had trusted each other. Their bubble of happiness had been pricked and had burst. Once burst, bubbles are gone for ever.

Sunk in a twilight zone of disappointment and bewilderment, she didn't open her eyes until a change in the sound of the car's engine alerted her to a change of speed. She looked out at a busy shopping street in a suburb of Milan. Tall tenement blocks soared up, skywards. People carrying umbrellas hurried along pavements. She looked at her watch. It was nearly a quarter to two. The car slid to a stop at a kerb in front of a *trattoria*.

They ate lunch like everyone else in that small but busy eating place, standing up at the counter, munching on thick pieces of Italian bread and slices of Parma ham and drinking *cappuccino*. They said nothing to each other. They didn't even look at each other. They could have been strangers. They were strangers, Sandra thought forlornly when they left and got into the car again.

To reach Portofino they didn't have to drive into the centre of Genoa but through suburbs to the south-bound coast road that twisted beside the amazingly blue Mediterranean. The steep slopes of the Ligurian Alps to the east seemed to want to push the road into the sea. They had to stop in a car park on the edge of Portofino because traffic wasn't allowed in the narrow streets of the little fishing village which clustered around the shores of a horseshoe-shaped harbour of sunset-tinted water where expensive-looking yachts were moored.

Leaving her in the car, Marco went to find out exactly the location of the Villa Montagna where Claire had told him she was staying.

'It's up in the hills,' he said when he returned.

'I wonder why she's come here?' queried Sandra, looking out at the thick vegetation of chestnut trees and cypresses as they drove along a road that twisted up the side of a hill in a series of hairpin bends. Everything was lush and still very green, the result of a mild climate.

Marco didn't answer her. He'd gone to his mountain top, Sandra thought with a wry grin at her own idea of him. Why had she ever thought they could be close friends? She had gone into marriage blindly, infatuated by him. not really knowing anything about him. She hadn't known, for instance, until he had told her today, what he had expected from marriage. She hadn't known he wanted more than being able to sleep with her and possess her physically. She hadn't realised he wanted from marriage the very things she wanted too.

The car swung between two stone gateposts and into a driveway edged with tall cypresses. The driveway ended in a courtyard before a house which had a square tower at one end. The house was painted pink and glowed in the last light of the setting sun. Yellow oblongs of windows glinted from under striped awnings.

'This is it. I don't see Claire rushing out to welcome you,' said Marco drily as he stopped the engine of the car.

They both got out of the car. Marco handed her case to her. Puzzled, she took it from him.

'I'll leave you now,' he said abruptly and turning back to the car he slid in behind the steering wheel, slamming the door closed. The engine started.

'But you can't leave like this!' exclaimed Sandra, rushing towards the car. She banged on the window beside him knowing he hadn't heard her. He glanced at her and rolled the window down.

'What's the matter?' he said.

'You can't leave me here like this. You can't just go

off,' she complained.

'I don't see why I shouldn't,' he replied coolly. 'I promised to bring you to see Claire and I've brought you. I don't have to stay around.'

'But don't you want to see Claire?'

'Not particularly.' He shrugged indifferently.

'But where will you go now?' She was stammering with bewilderment. She hadn't expected him to behave like this.

'Do you really care about where I go?' he taunted. 'I'm going back to Genoa. I have to meet someone there.'

'Then you didn't come all this way just for me?' she whispered, feeling the chill of rejection creeping through her. He didn't answer her but revved the engine impatiently, looking away from her, into the increasing gloom. 'So when shall I see you again?' she added quickly.

'That's up to you,' he replied. 'I'll be going back to Venice tomorrow. How long will you be staying here?'

'I have to be back in London by Monday morning. I'll probably fly back from Genoa on Sunday,' she said stiffly, pride stepping in, coming between them.

'I see,' he murmured. 'Then perhaps you'll let me know before the end of the year what it is you want to do. That will give you six weeks to make a decision.'

'What decision?' she asked weakly.

'About a divorce. Either we divorce or you agree to come back to Venice to live with me,' he replied. 'I've told you what I want in a wife, what I expect from you.'

'You want to possess me,' she hissed.

'Exactly,' he retorted with a brief glinting glance in

her direction. '*Buona sera*, Sandra. And thanks for coming.'

He revved the engine again, the window began to roll up and she stepped back quickly. The car's tyres churned up gravel as it shot forward and, suppressing a desire to run after it, Sandra stood watching the rear lights glow brighter as Marco braked for a bend in the drive; watching him drive out of her life.

Picking up her case again, she walked towards the front door of the villa and up a flight of shallow steps.

An Italian woman with sleek black hair drawn back tightly from her forehead answered the ringing of the bell. She was dressed in a neat black dress with white cuffs and collar and Sandra guessed she was a housekeeper.

'I've come to see the contessa Fontelli. Is she at home?' she asked the woman in Italian.

'There is no Contessa here,' the woman replied. 'You are at the wrong house.'

'This is the Villa Montagna, isn't it?'

'*Si*. You are right.'

'Then she must be here. The Contessa Fontelli, I mean,' asserted Sandra speaking in English then repeating what she had said in Italian. 'She phoned me from this address.' She groped in her handbag and brought out the piece of paper on which she had written Claire's phone number. 'Look. Isn't this the phone number of the house?' she asked, showing the woman the paper.

'*Si, si*.' The woman nodded vigorously. 'But no contessa stay here. I am housekeeper here for Signor Edmonds, an Englishman. I know no Contessa Fontelli live here or visit here.'

'Then where is she?'

'I do not know, *signora*. *Bouna sera*.

The woman stepped back and closed the door. Sandra, utterly mystified, stood and stared at the lighted glass panels of the door and was tempted to ring again and demand to see Signor Edmonds. But something about the conviction with which the housekeeper had spoken decided her against taking such a course. Picking up her case again she went down the steps and began to walk along the driveway.

Where was Claire? How could she find out where Claire was? If only Marco hadn't been in such a hurry to leave her and go back to Genoa, had waited to see if Claire had been at the villa.

He had gone to meet someone. Whom? Whom was he meeting there? Couldn't be Lucia, surely. Another woman, then? One she hadn't heard about? Jealous suspicion crawled through her mind as she wandered down the driveway.

The way was dark, the air soft and scented with pine trees and cypresses. It was very quiet up there high on the hillside. All she could hear was the distant drone of a car's engine coming up the hill from the village.

At the end of the driveway she stopped to rest. Her case was much heavier than she had thought. How many miles was it to the village? And what would she do when she got there? Again she found herself wishing that Marco hadn't left her in such a hurry. He had behaved as if he hadn't cared what happened to her, as if their marriage was over already. He had loved her until last night, he had said, until she had walked out of the dinner party. He felt she had let him down. It looked as if she had only herself to blame for his sudden turning off.

Perhaps neither of them had loved the other properly. Her love for him had collapsed like a pricked balloon when she had found out about Lucia. His love for her, lasting a little longer than hers for him, had been snuffed out like the flame of a candle, only last night.

He had loved her until last night. Then why hadn't he told her when he had been making love to her? Had he thought it enough to kiss her and possess her physically? If he had explained about Lucia instead of making love to her she wouldn't have been upset when Lucia had arrived at the dinner party. And she wouldn't be here now, standing on this corner, feeling deserted and wondering where to go next. Never had she felt so forlorn.

Light from two approaching headlamps streamed over her. The car she had heard coming up the hill was very close now. She picked up her case and began to walk towards it going down the hill. The powerful beams of light were so dazzling she had to stop to wait at the side of the road for the car to pass. When it drew level with her she recognised the distinctive outline of a Rolls-Royce bonnet. Much to her surprise, the car stopped right beside her. The nearest window was rolled down and a pale triangle of a woman's face looked out at her.

'Sandra, darling,' Claire exclaimed. 'What are you doing here? Why aren't you in the villa waiting for us?'

Suppressing a forthright desire to demand of Claire why she hadn't been waiting at the villa for her daughter's arrival, Sandra stepped forward and said, 'The housekeeper said you weren't staying in the villa. She said Contessa Fontelli wasn't there and had never been there.'

Laughter interrupted her, Claire's infectious trill and a man's laugh, gruff but by no means unpleasant.

Sandra peered beyond Claire's head, trying to see him.

'But of course, she doesn't know me by that name,' drawled Claire. 'Get in the car, darling, and I'll explain everything when we get to the house. We knew you had arrived. We met Marco at the bottom of the hill and he said he'd left you at the villa. What a good thing we came back from Genoa when we did. We might have missed you if we hadn't.'

CHAPTER SIX

THE back seat of the Rolls was wide and engulfing. Sandra sank into its thick-cushioned comfort gratefully, leaned back and stared at the top of the head of the man who was driving. That was all she could see of him, a dark shape in the shadowy interior of the car.

The Rolls floated forward, turned into the driveway and drove up to the pink villa. It stopped and the engine was switched off. The driver got out and went round to open the door beside Claire, who stepped out without a word of thanks to him. He closed that door and opened the door beside Sandra.

'I'm Harry Edmonds,' he said pleasantly, with a slightly Welsh lilt to his voice. 'Hop out and go in with Claire. I'll bring your case. Nice to meet you at last, Sandra.'

'Harry and I were married last week and we've come here for our honeymoon,' said Claire, taking hold of Sandra's arm and leading her towards the steps. 'You understand now, perhaps, why I didn't want you to come here.' Claire laughed again. 'You'll understand, too, why the housekeeper, Signora Petuli, told you she didn't know of Contesssa Fontelli. She knows me only as Signora Edmonds.'

Claire, married again? It was another shock, and Sandra was sure she staggered with surprise. As if at a signal, the front door opened again as soon as she and Claire reached the top step. Signora Petuli smiled at

Claire but her eyebrows shot up in surprise when she recognised Sandra.

'This is my daughter, Signora Petuli,' Claire explained quickly. 'Her name is Morosini, Signora Morosini, and she will be staying with us for a couple of nights.'

Signora Petuli nodded her head and smiled at Sandra, apologising for not knowing who she was earlier. Claire explained the easily-made mistake and drew Sandra with her into a long room furnished comfortably as a lounge. Harry Edmonds was close behind them, having left Sandra's case with the housekeeper.

'So how about a drink, to make Sandra welcome?' he said cheerfully. Tall and lean, he had thick, wavy, greyish-brown hair and observant hazel eyes.

'Sounds good to me,' said Claire, sinking down with her usual grace in the corner of a cream-coloured settee. 'Sit here, Sandra, near me. I expect you've heard of Harry, if you watch TV drama at all. He's a playwright and script-writer for films. We met years ago, when I was in repertory and he was a struggling writer.'

'What would you like to drink, Sandra?' asked Harry. She chose a glass of white wine and Claire selected gin and tonic. Harry went over to a drinks cabinet in a corner of the room.

'Still in a state of shock, darling?' Claire teased Sandra.

'Er, yes, in a way! Why didn't you tell me when we spoke on the phone last night?'

'Well, actually I thought you'd know. I thought Marco would tell you.'

'Marco doesn't tell me anything,' muttered Sandra bitterly.

'Oh. Like that, is it?' remarked Claire shrewdly. 'When we saw him in the village Harry invited him to come back here and stay for the night, but he refused, said something about having an appointment to keep in Genoa.'

'Here you are.' Harry came over to them with their drinks on a small silver tray. 'Welcome, Sandra,' he said, raising his own glass in a toast to her. 'You've no idea how pleased I am to be presented with a ready-made, grown-up daughter.'

'Thank you,' said Sandra, smiling wanly, gulping back an urgent desire to burst into tears. She picked up her glass of wine. 'Congratulations to both of you,' she murmured.

She glanced at Claire, felt a sudden upsurge of affection for her and, setting down her untasted glass of wine, flung herself forward, her arms going around Claire to hug her.

'Oh, Mother.' It was the first time she had ever called Claire 'mother'. 'I'm so unhappy,' she whispered, and let the tears come.

'Well, really, darling.' Claire, for once, sounded disconcerted. 'I'm sorry to hear it.'

Sandra pushed free, sniffing and groping for a handkerchief.

'I'm sorry,' she muttered and glanced sideways at Harry. 'I didn't mean to cry. What I meant to say was I'm happy for both of you. Happy you're married. It . . . it came out all wrong.'

'It probably came out all *right*,' said Harry consolingly. 'Your deepest feeling at the moment is one of unhappiness so you expressed it. And so you should. Tell Claire all about it while I go and do some telephoning. See you later, at dinner. You too, my love.' He bent over Claire and kissed her, then left the room.

'He seems to be very kind,' said Sandra after blowing her nose. 'When did you meet him again?'

'Last April, when I was in Monaco. It was such a surprise. Of course I knew he'd been successful but I'd no idea he was able to afford a place like this. He hardly ever lives in England now.' Claire laughed a little. 'I'd no idea either that he'd been keen on me all those years ago, when I first knew him. It's really quite a romance, darling. Harry had never married because he'd never found another woman like me, so when we met again he lost no time in proposing. And I . . . well, I was only too happy to accept.'

'You look very well. Not at all as if you'd been in a car accident,' said Sandra. Claire's face was, as always, perfectly made up and her hair was a froth of silver-gilt curls. A suit with a pleated skirt and a long-line jacket, made from lilac wool, flattered her figure and set off her fair colouring.

'It was only a little accident really, but we thought we should inform Alfredo about it. I suppose he told Marco. But I didn't ask *anyone* to ask you to come and see me. That must have been Marco's own idea.' A slight and rather mysterious smile curved over Claire's lips. 'He really is as devious as the devil, isn't he? Quite fascinating, I've always found him, and there have been times, I don't mind admitting, when I've wished he'd been a little older or I had been a little younger, especially after Francesco's death when we were thrown into each other's company so much.' Claire sighed. 'I really don't know what I'd have done without Marco then. He was a tower of strength, and so kind and so thoughtful. But he only saw me as a nuisance, one that Francesco had wished on to him. He made no bones about his relief when I told him I wanted to marry Harry, and he suggested immediately that I sell the shares Francesco left me.'

'Marco suggested you sell them?' exclaimed Sandra.

'Yes, so that I could resign the chairmanship. Harry only wanted to marry me on condition that I gave up any interest in Fontelli's. He said he wanted me all to himself and didn't want to share me with my late husband's company. I could see his point, and so could Marco, thank heavens. He arranged it all. Got his uncle to buy some of the shares and took the rest himself. I suppose he told you Ian Morison is now chairman.'

'Yes, he did. I met Ian and Liza last night. Claire, why did you never tell me about them? You must have met them, known them.'

'Didn't I tell you?' queried Claire airily. 'Oh, well, it doesn't matter, now, does it? I suppose I didn't think either worth mentioning to you. Liza and I never got on well together and I always had the impression Ian didn't approve of me either. They resented me because Francesco married me, I think, and because he made me his heiress.' Claire finished her drink and set the glass down on the tray. 'But I want to know about you and Marco. What is going on? I'd like to know why you left him in April for a start.'

'I left him because I thought . . . I mean, I thought I'd found out that he'd been deceiving me,' muttered Sandra.

'You thought you'd found out . . . What on earth do you mean? In what way did you think you'd found out he had been deceiving you? Oh, how crazy it sounds, and how like you, you scatterbrain!' Claire was openly critical.

'Someone told me that he had married me only because I'm your daughter,' said Sandra and thought how silly her answer seemed.

'So. Perhaps he did. But I remember you told me you wanted to tell him you're my daughter and I suggested you didn't at the time. How did he find out?'

'I don't know. He said he guessed I was.'

'Well, what's wrong with him marrying you because you're my daughter?' snapped Claire impatiently.

'You were the chairman of Fontelli's at the time and owned most of the shares.'

'Oh, I see. This someone you talk about suggested Marco was feathering his own nest by marrying you. Is that it?'

'Yes.'

'Mmm,' murmured Claire thoughtfully. 'Could be the someone was right there. One of the reasons I didn't want anyone to know you were my daughter was to protect you from fortune-hunters, although I have to admit I would never have put Marco in that category. Who was this someone you refer to?'

'Lucia Spenola.'

'Oh, God,' said Claire succinctly, and seemed to collapse against the arm of the settee.

'Why do you say that?' demanded Sandra. 'Do you know Lucia?'

'I've met her. She's Liza's daughter by her first husband and Liza tried to arrange a marriage between Lucia and Marco some years ago, when he was in the States. It came to nothing but that didn't stop Lucia from regarding him as her own particular property. I suppose she let you know that too.'

'She . . . she implied that she was his mistress,' mumbled Sandra.

'And you believed her. Oh, you stupid little goose. I suppose you went flying to Marco then and accused him of cheating on you?'

'Yes, I did. And he didn't deny it.'

'So you left. Oh, my God,' groaned Claire. 'You're just like Charlton, acting on impulse all the time, flying off the handle. And I always thought Marco had the measure of you, could cope with your naïveté, your flashes of temper.'

'But can't you understand how I felt?' cried Sandra. 'Could you have stayed with a man when you found out he had married you not for love but for what you might inherit from your mother one day? When you found out he was having an affair with another woman?'

'I could forgive him for marrying me for what I might inherit one day. After all I married Francesco because he was wealthy and I was tired of being poor,' replied Claire slowly. 'As for the other . . . I think I'd have stayed and asked a few more questions about this so-called affair between him and Lucia. Oh, I wouldn't have stood around submissively either. I'd have given him hell. But I wouldn't have run away. I'd have hung in there until I was damned sure he wasn't seeing the other woman again, especially if I were his wife and I loved him. Do you love Marco?'

Sandra looked down at her empty glass, twiddled it round.

'I . . . I'm not sure,' she whispered.

'You were *in* love with him when you married him, anyone could see that,' drawled Claire. 'Talk about starry-eyed, and all through those first months, too. But you shouldn't have left him, and if I'd been in

Venice at the time I'd have talked you out of leaving. He's very proud, you know, and you hurt his pride when you skipped out. I doubt if he'll ever forgive you. I'm really rather surprised he tricked you into returning to Venice yesterday, but I suppose you jumped at the chance to see him again, hoping he would let bygones by bygones . . .'

'No, I didn't.' Sandra was indignant. 'I really believed you were badly hurt. He tricked me into believing that. He's always tricking me. If he'd been honest right from the start and told me everything about himself . . .' She broke off and glanced at Claire who was watching her with an expression of rather pitying amusement. 'Do you know who Marco's father is or was?' she demanded.

'My God, does it matter?' Claire now looked bored. 'Do you?'

'Sometimes I've suspected who he was, but if you want to know so badly why don't you ask Marco himself? I'm sure he'll tell you, if he knows. Has he ever asked you about your father?'

'No. But that's different.'

'Is it? I don't see why it's different.'

Defeated by this sharp rebuke, Sandra put her glass down. Talking to Claire wasn't easing the feeling of desolation which had claimed her ever since Marco had mentioned divorce. She now had a feeling she had made a terrible mistake, as if she had thrown away something of great value which could have been hers for ever if she hadn't been so impetuous and run away from Marco; if she had been less infatuated by the idea of *him* being in love with *her* and had loved him more truly for himself.

'I've made an awful mess of everything,' she muttered.

'And I can't help but agree with you, darling,' said Claire coolly. 'But that's a start in the right direction. It always helps to admit you've been in the wrong. Would you like to tell me what else you've done in the short time you've been in Italy? I gather whatever it is hasn't improved the relationship between you and Marco. He would be here with you if it had, and not in Genoa. What have you done to offend him now?'

Haltingly, Sandra described all that had happened since she arrived at Venice airport the previous afternoon, leaving out only the lovemaking between herself and Marco.

'So you believed he had invited Lucia and were so furious you left,' remarked Claire thoughtfully. She glanced at Sandra. 'Going by your previous impetuous behaviour, that doesn't surprise me. But do you still believe that she's his mistress even though he has told you she isn't?'

'It's very hard to know what to believe,' sighed Sandra. 'And now he thinks I stayed the night with Giulio. We just don't trust each other any more, and before he left me here he said he'll give me six weeks until the end of the year to decide whether I want a divorce or not.'

'How like Marco to issue an ultimatum,' said Claire. 'Reminds me of Francesco.' She frowned slightly. 'He was always issuing them. But Marco has been very generous in the amount of time he's given you to make up your mind. I'd have thought he would have insisted on you making up your mind before you leave Italy. When are you leaving, by the way?'

'I have to be back at work by Monday morning. I've told you that already.'

'So you have, so you have.' Claire leaned forward, chin on her hand, elbow on her knee in a pose of thoughtfulness, the frown still there as she stared into the middle distance. 'I wonder,' she said slowly. 'I just wonder if Liza and Ian have been putting pressure on Marco to divorce you.'

'Why would they do that?'

'So that he'd be free to marry Lucia, of course. It's quite possible that you were set up last night at that dinner party, by Liza.'

'But she was so friendly. She was charming,' protested Sandra.

'She's a Fontelli, darling,' remarked Claire drily. 'Charm is their middle name and deceit their second middle name. They thrive on intrigue. Liza has always wanted Marco for her beloved daughter, firstly because he's wealthy and secondly because he is the power behind the throne at Fontelli's since Francesco died. As I see it, based on what I know of you and of Liza and Lucia, Lucia met you in April, sized you up for what you are—a gullible romantic and a little unsure of yourself. She dropped hints about an affair she once had with Marco and, reacting just as she hoped, you flew the coop.'

'You really think she lied to me about her relationship with Marco, then?' asked Sandra.

'It's very possible. You stayed in England. Everything seemed to be going Lucia's way, and then suddenly you were back again, in Venice attending a dinner party with Marco as if celebrating your reconciliation. Knowing how you were likely to react to Lucia's sudden arrival at the party, Liza invited her. The rest is history,' Claire gestured airily. 'And if you go back to London now you'll play right into their hands.'

'But what else can I do?' said Sandra.

'Stay here with us, at least until Sunday. That's the only advice I dare give you. Stay here; it's quiet, peaceful, and mull the matter over. I guess you're no less in love with Marco than you were when you married him . . .'

'But he doesn't love me,' Sandra pointed out.

'Let me finish, darling, please,' Claire rebuked her gently. 'I guess you're still in love with him, and if you are you'll go to Venice on Sunday and not to London.'

'No, no. You're wrong. I'll never go back to Venice. Never. I can't.'

'In that case, I'm afraid Lucia and Liza have won already and your marriage to Marco is finished. I doubt very much if he'll make any more moves to get you back, considering what has happened during the last twenty-four hours. He won't be following you to London. You can forget that. And you don't really deserve that he should. He's fed up with you, that's becoming very clear.'

Claire rose gracefully to her feet. Feeling she had just plumbed the very depths of despair, Sandra continued to sit where she was, shoulders sagging, lips drooping.

'Well, that's enough of that,' said Claire more cheerfully. 'Let's get to more important things. We'll go up to the room where you're going to sleep tonight. You can take a shower and change. You look like a week of wet Fridays,' she mocked. 'Come on, where's your backbone?' As Sandra stood up, Claire's blue gaze drifted critically over the emerald-green dress. 'I wonder what on earth posseessed you to travel in that dress,' she remarked and sighed. 'You know, sometimes I wonder if you really are my child or if you're a changeling, your sense of dress is appalling.'

'Oh, you're as bad as Marco. He's always on about

my clothes. It's one of the arguments we're always having. He seems to think I should dress to please him. Oh, Mother, what's the use? He and I aren't compatible, you know.'

'Neither were Charlton and I,' retorted Claire. 'But we loved each other enough to get over that. We disagreed on most subjects but, oh, how exciting it was to be with him. Never a dull moment.'

They went upstairs to a small suite of rooms at the back of the house. Sandra's case was already in the bedroom.

'Let me see what you have to wear for dinner,' Claire said autocratically. 'Unlock your case.'

'I have only a suit with me apart from this dress. I didn't bring much with me. I didn't think I'd be away for long,' Sandra said defensively.

'Then I'll see what I have that might fit you. You can't possibly come down to dinner in that dress. It needs cleaning and pressing.'

Claire left the room and Sandra went into the bathroom, remembering unexpectedly the previous evening when she had barged in on Marco just as he had been leaving the shower. Inevitably her thoughts strayed on to what had happened afterwards, and before long she was groaning in the agony of misery, because it was beginning to look as if it would never happen again. In a few short minutes she had destroyed his love for her by walking out of Mario's restaurant.

Was it possible that Liza had set her up, arranged for Lucia to be at that party to upset her deliberately and make her run away from Marco again? Claire's assessment of what had happened seemed to fit in with Marco's suggestion that Lucia had turned up out of spite to make another attempt to destroy his marriage.

The more she thought about it, the more tangled and sinister the situation seemed, and quite beyond her powers to deal with. As Claire pointed out, she was a gullible romantic with no understanding of family intrigue, and was easily manipulated by such experts as Liza and Lucia, to say nothing of Marco.

When she had showered and dried herself she returned to the bedroom wearing her dressing-gown. Claire was already there with several of her own dresses. She held each one of them up against Sandra to regard the effect critically.

'This navy-blue chiffon will look best,' she said at last. 'I'll go and put the rest away. Get dressed in it and I'll come back to see if it needs any adjustment.' She flashed Sandra a bright smile over her shoulder. 'Safety pins,' she said. 'You'd be surprised how many of the best-dressed women in the world are pinned into their clothes with safety pins.'

The dress was simple, high-necked and ruffled, with a gathered skirt. The length was just right but it was too wide.

'You're much thinner than you were,' remarked Claire as she adjusted the waistline, tucking it with a couple of safety pins. 'Too thin, I would say. I guess you've been pining for Marco without knowing it.'

'No, I haven't,' Sandra asserted indignantly but uncertainly. 'I've been getting along perfectly well without him. I have a good job, nice friends and I've been busy all summer. I haven't had time to pine,'

'Then you must have been dieting.' Claire clicked her tongue and frowned severely as she stepped back to look at the dress. 'I hope you're not going to get anorexia nervosa. It's not worth it, you know, being too thin. And I haven't met a man yet who didn't like a woman to have a few curves.' She wiggled her hips and flaunted her bosom in Mae West style. 'They like something to get hold of and fondle.' She went off into a peal of laughter. 'Oh, don't look so shocked, darling. What a prude you are. I've often wondered what a hot-blooded sophisticate like Marco has ever seen in you.'

'I've wondered the same thing,' muttered Sandra, with sudden insight into her own insecurity. 'That's why I've always been unsure of him. That's why it was easy to believe Lucia when she insinuated that he had only married me because I was related to the biggest shareholder in Fontelli's. And now you're not the biggest shareholder so he has no reason to stay married to me, and yesterday he said that if I decide to end our separation and go back to him he'll think I want to stay married to to him because . . . oh, because he's wealthy and his uncle is chairman.'

'He was probably only teasing you, darling,' Claire comforted her. 'Now, if we tie the belt just so, no one will guess you're pinned into this dress.' Claire laughed again. 'Not that there's anyone to guess except Harry and the maid and Signora Petuli.'

Thinking that as usual clothes and appearances were more important to Claire than her own daughter's feelings, Sandra followed her mother downstairs. She loved Claire dearly, she thought, but not because she was related to her or because she was kind and comforting, giving her moral support without question as Joan would have done—as a mother was supposed to do. In fact, in this matter of conflict between herself and Marco, Claire seemed to be more on his side than on hers. Claire preferred Marco to her. Because he was a man? Probably. Claire had never hidden the fact that she preferred the opposite sex to her own.

Just before they entered the dining-room, Claire paused. 'Now, no long faces this evening, darling. Remember, Harry and I are on our honeymoon and you wouldn't be here if I'd had my way. Unfortunately when Marco called this morning and asked if he could bring you to see me Harry took the call and agreed to let you come. So I'd like you to make an effort to smile and be agreeable. This is one little dinner party you're not going to leave if something happens or is said that you don't like. You know I really think Joan and Ed have spoilt you, have let you have your own way too much.'

'They've always been very kind to me,' muttered Sandra.

'Too kind, I suspect,' retorted Claire smoothly. 'Too protective. They've sheltered you from everything and you've had no chance to learn the skills of self-defence.'

It wasn't hard to smile and be agreeable with Harry. He was a jovial host, entertaining her with anecdotes of his experiences as a playwright and script-writer for films, but inevitably he came round to the reason for her being at the villa.

'Claire has been telling me about your problems with Marco,' he said. 'You seem to behave very impetuously. Are you always like that?'

'She's like Charlton, Harry,' remarked Claire. 'And you know what he was like.'

'Oh, did you know my father?' exclaimed Sandra.

'I certainly did,' said Harry with a sly grimace. 'He was my rival for your mother's affections years ago. He won.'

'I wish you'd tell me something about him,' said

Sandra, glancing apologetically at Claire. 'Claire has told me a little but not enough. You've no idea what it's like not knowing about your own parents.'

'I can understand, though,' Harry said kindly. 'It's a form of anxiety all adopted children suffer from, so I'm told, no matter how good at parenting their adoptive parents are. Well, for your information, although there were times when I hated his guts and was as jealous as hell of him, Charlton Lewis, your father, was one of the most lovable people I've ever known. Do you mind if I tell her about Charlie, Claire? About my opinion of him, that is. It might help her to understand herself a little?'

'No, I don't mind. Go ahead,' said Claire. 'It might help me to understand Charlie and Claire a little better too.'

'He was first and foremost an actor, dedicated to his profession; it's important to remember that,' said Harry. 'Nothing else mattered to him seriously. But he had a mercurial disposition. He was always changing his mind and rushing into situations without a thought for the consequences. Does that sound familiar?' Harry cocked a mocking eyebrow as he looked at Sandra, who shifted uncomfortably on her chair.

'It certainly does,' drawled Claire.

'He wasn't what you would call a family man, wasn't interested in being married or tied down, but I believe he loved Claire in his own way and he was delighted when you were born.' Harry leaned forward, his lean, lined face serious. 'He'd want to try and help you now, Sandra, and I hope you'll let me take his place for a few minutes. Don't let your marriage break up yet. You and Marco haven't been married long, and too many marriages break up these days over small disagreements and misunderstandings.'

'Then, like Claire, you think I should go back to Venice instead of returning to London,' said Sandra, avoiding his intent stare.

'I think you should seriously see whether there is anything to gain by returning to London,' he replied. 'Are you hoping Marco will follow you there? Isn't that why you keep running away from him?'

'Perhaps,' she admitted reluctantly.

'In the same way Charlton used to stalk off the stage and go to the nearest pub whenever he thought the director of any play he was acting in was criticising him too much or asking too much of him. Charlie couldn't argue. He could only show by his reactions how he felt.'

'How right you are, Harry!' said Claire with a little clap of her hands. 'Charlie would get all steamed up and walk away from some of the best chances he ever had. He seemed to think that he was indispensable to any repertory company he performed with and was quite put out when his behaviour was ignored and they found someone else to act in a part from which he had deliberately walked away.'

'He always hoped, you see, that the director would follow him, go down on his bended knees and plead with him to go back to the stage and rehearse the part.' Harry shook his head sadly. 'Poor Charlie, how many times he was disappointed and lost his job.' Harry flashed Sandra another penetrating glance. 'You see what I'm getting at?' he enquired.

'I think so,' she muttered.

There was no more talk about the situation between her and Marco, nor about Charlton Lewis, her father. Having had their say, Claire and Harry seemed quite happy to forget Sandra's problems. Harry even offered to phone an airline and book her a seat on a flight from Genoa to London on Sunday, when Claire told him that Sandra would be leaving on that day.

Sandra went to bed feeling far better than she had expected to feel, and slept better than she had ever expected to sleep that night, but when she woke up on Saturday morning her thoughts were full of Marco and what she should do to prevent their marriage from breaking up.

Would she gain anything by returning to London? Harry and Claire seemed to think that Marco wouldn't follow her there. He had given her until the end of the year to come to a decision. She counted up on her fingers. Today was the second week of November. She had just over six weeks to make up her mind.

What would she do during that time? Go to work, go back to the flat she shared with Thea every night. Visit Joan and Ed at the weekends. Occasionally, when and if he invited her, go to a concert or a film with Kevin Collins. A drab routine when compared to living with Marco.

Wouldn't it be best to go back to Venice tomorrow? At the thought, excitement flooded through her. She imagined how Marco might greet her, the lovemaking that would take place, and immediately she was writhing on the bed, aching for the touch of his lips, the subtle titillation of his fingers seeking and finding sensitive and responsive nerves. She longed for him to be there in the bed with her, stroking her, holding her closely to his vibrant body. She wanted him and no other lover. No one else could take his place. She realised that now she was in danger of having lost him.

Her thoughts were interrupted by the arrival of the maid with her breakfast. The blinds were raised and sunlight streamed into the room. As she ate, Sandra

looked round the pretty room and thought of the
bedroom in Marco's apartment, its richness and
comfort. Then she thought of her bedroom in the
London flat, how narrow and small it was, not big
enough for all her belongings.

If she went back to Marco, stayed married to him,
comfort and luxury would always be hers. Wasn't that
a good enough reason to give in and return to Venice?
She knew it would have been a good enough reason for
Claire.

But not for her. She had to have more from Marco
than an allowance, clothes and comfort. She had to
know that no other woman mattered as much to him
as she did. She had to have his promise that he would
never again see Lucia. She couldn't return to him
unconditionally . . .

So didn't that mean she didn't really love him?

Oh, it was hopeless. She would never be able to
reach a thought-out decision. Logic wasn't her strong
suit, and apparently it hadn't been her father's, either.
She acted, she didn't think. Or rather she reacted, her
reactions springing from strongly felt emotions. If
only something would happen to make her react. If
only Marco would change his mind and instead of
going back to Venice today come back to the villa, tell
her he couldn't live without her and make her go back
with him. Her eyes closed tightly, her hands gripped
together, she prayed for that to happen, and then she
got up.

The morning passed pleasantly for her in Harry's
company. He drove her down to the village where they
walked along a narrow street to the square by the
harbour. The weather was calm and mild. The
terraces of colour-washed narrow houses crowding
close to the water were reflected perfectly in the

smooth harbour as were the sleek white hulls of yachts and powerboats. In the pale yet warm sunshine they sat under a tree outside a café in the square and sipped *espresso*, then returned to the villa.

After lunch, Claire and Harry disappeared. Sandra decided to climb the hill at the back of the house, taking a pathway that twisted through the thick woods, until she reached a level place where the land belonging to the villa was fenced off from that belonging to the next villa and where someone had thoughtfully placed a wooden bench.

She sat on the bench for a while to admire the view of shimmering blue sea, lush green foliage covering hills, and rocky headlands. Here there were no dank marshes or lagoons, no satanic chimneys and no industrial waste. But there was no magical city either, glittering pink and gold in the sunlight.

The sun had begun to slide towards the horizon and the air temperature was growing cooler before she decided to leave that place and return to the house. She hadn't reached any decision as to what she would do and was beginning to accept that she never would by *thinking*. She would just drift on the way she was until something happened. Then she would act.

But supposing nothing happens? chided an inner voice. What then?

She was still slightly above the house on the hillside but with a clear view of the courtyard and the driveway when she saw a car drive into the space before the house and stop. It was an ordinary, compact car. She stopped walking and watched. A door of the car opened and a man got out. He was tall and big-shouldered, dressed in tweeds. He walked round to the other side of the car, opened the front door. A woman stepped out, a woman with frizzy black hair. Lucia Spenola.

Sandra stared. What was Lucia doing here? Why had she come to the Villa Montagna? Had she heard that Marco would be here and had she followed him? As she stared, Lucia and the man disappeared from her view to go up to the front door, presumably, and another car, a bigger car more like a limousine, nosed its way out of the driveway into the courtyard. It also stopped. A uniformed chauffeur got out and opened one of the rear doors. First Liza and then Ian Morison got out. They also disappeared from her view as they went towards the house,

What were they all doing here? Why had they come? Rushing into action, Sandra ran the rest of the way to the house and entered by the same side door through which she had left. Within a few minutes she was in the passageway on the second floor, having gone up there by a back staircase, and was tiptoeing towards the landing at the top of the main stairs which overlooked the entrance hall. Quietly she approached the carved wooden railings at the edge of the landing and looked down.

Lucia, the strange man, Liza and Ian were standing in the hall waiting, she assumed for their arrival to be announced to Harry by Signora Petuli. In a short time Harry appeared, striding into the hall from the direction of his study. He greeted them in his cheerful hospitable way, shaking hands with the two men when they introduced themselves. Then he began to usher them all towards the living-room. Something of what he was saying floated up to Sandra. She distinctly heard him say, 'Marco? No, he isn't here. No, he didn't stay the night. You'd like to see Claire, though, I'm sure. Please, come in and make yourselves comfortable . . .'

His voice faded. Turning away, Sandra walked along to her bedroom suite, went in and closed the door. She would stay there until they had gone, she decided. Once they had seen Claire, once they knew that Marco wasn't expected back at the villa they would leave, wouldn't they? But why had they come?

She was sitting trying to read a novel she had taken from the bookcase in the small sitting-room and thinking she would have to put a light on because the sun was setting and the room was growing dark, when there was a knock on the door. She went to open it. Signora Petuli was outside, placid and poker-faced.

'The *signor* and signora request that you join them in the lounge for cocktails,' she announced.

'Oh. Is anyone with them? Do they have guests?' asked Sandra cautiously.

'*Si*. Signor and Signora Morison and Signorina Spenola and and other *signor* whose name I do not understand.'

'Thank you.' Sandra nodded and began to close the door.

'They will be staying to dinner too,' added Signora Petuli.

'All of them?' Sandra queried.

'*Si*, all of them,' replied the housekeeper. 'You will come down now, to the lounge?'

'No, I don't think so. Please ask them to excuse me.'

The housekeeper marched away and Sandra closed the door. Switching on a standard lamp she sat down again. Nothing was going to make her go down and join Lucia, Liza and Ian and a stranger for drinks. Nothing. She wasn't going to have dinner with them either. Her feelings about Lucia hadn't changed at all.

She was still jealous of the woman for having known Marco before she had, no matter how innocent their affair might have been and she still blamed Lucia for destroying her trust in Marco. She would stay up there in her room until they left even if it meant being hungry ...

But why should she stay? Why not leave? Hardly had the idea occurred to her than she went into action, stuffing her few clothes and belongings in her case. She zipped it up, put on her raincoat over her suit, wrote a brief note for Claire which she left on the dressing table, just four words which would tell everything to Claire: Have gone to Venice.

Down the back stairs she ran out into the night, along the driveway, dark and scented as on the previous evening. But how different her feelings were. Then she had been uncertain and unhappy because Marco had just deserted her. Now she felt almost joyful because she had come, surprisingly to a decision. She was going back to Venice and Marco. It was going to be hard to face him and to admit she had been wrong, but she was going to do it. She was going to tell him she was willing to start all over again.

Along the driveway she hurried, her case banging against her legs yet with never a thought for the weight of it. She was in the middle of the driveway and about to run out into the road when she heard a car coming up the hill fast. Her shoes skidding on the gravel she stopped her headlong career forwards but had no time to get out of the way of the car. White light from headlamps blinded her as the car swung with a squeal of tyres into the driveway. She flung herself sideways, letting go of her case. She felt something nudge her hip and then she was down and rolling to the side of the driveway.

Shaking from the shock of falling Sandra managed to get on all fours, kneeling with her arms supporting her. Vaguely she was aware that the car had stopped. A door slammed and she heard quick footsteps coming towards her. A voice spoke to her imperatively in Italian asking her if she were hurt. To her amazement the voice sounded exactly like Marco's.

'Oh, why do you always have to drive so fast?' she complained breathlessly. 'Why couldn't you have slowed down for that corner? Who do you think you are when you get in a car? Your friend, Tony Manzini?'

'Sandra?' He squatted down beside her. 'What are you doing here? Where are you going now? Running away again?' Scorn edged his voice but his hands were gentle as they took hold of hers and helped her stand up to face him. Since she swayed a little he kept hold of her hands. By the light blazing from the car's headlamps she could see he was frowning. Sparks of icy light glittered at her from between his eyelashes. Then suddenly he had hold of her shoulders and was shaking her, as if she hadn't been shaken enough.

'You bloody little fool,' he rasped. 'You might have been killed! Why don't you look where you're going? Why are you always running away?'

He stopped shaking her and pulled her roughly against him, his arms tightly around her, holding her as if he would never let her go. And she wished he wouldn't. She wished he would hold her forever like that as she gave in and leaned against him.

CHAPTER SEVEN

SHE didn't exactly faint, but everything swayed around her and she was forced to cling to him. She was aware that he was speaking to her but was unable to make out what he was saying because her head seemed to be filled with a grey fog as thick as cotton wool that made hearing as well as seeing difficult.

Then she seemed to be floating through the air. Her feet were off the ground anyway. The fog cleared suddenly and she knew he was carrying her. He set her down beside the car and, keeping an arm around her, opened a door. Gently he pushed her down on to the front passenger seat. When he squatted down in front of her she could see by the light thrown back from the headlamps, which were still on, that his face was pale, new lines having been graven in his cheeks and about his lips, and that he was frowning. He reached out as if to lift her legs up and around into the car.

'It's all right. I'm all right now. Really,' she whispered. 'Could you get my case, please? I dropped it when I tried to get out of the way.'

'I'll get it. First I want you to sit properly and I'll fasten the seat belt around you,' he said briskly.

She turned and lifted her legs into the space before her. He leaned across her to fasten the seat belt and she stiffened involuntarily, jerking back, afraid that his face might touch hers and that, feeling the warmth and strength of him again, so close to her now that she was more alert, she might break down and plead with him to hold her again and comfort her.

'Do you hurt anywhere?' he asked, when the belt was fastened and he was squatting back on his heels. 'Your legs seem to be all right or you wouldn't have stood up so easily when I helped you.'

'I think I may have a few bruises, that's all. And I've ruined my raincoat and my tights.'

'Those can soon be replaced. But you can't,' he whispered and stretching out a hand he ran a finger caressingly down her cheek. '*Cara,*' he began, his voice deepening.

'Please,' she muttered shakily. 'Please, Marco, don't. I . . . I . . .'

Her voice failed but he withdrew his hand quickly, stood up and swung the door shut with a slam as if her rejection of his touch had annoyed him. In a few seconds he was opening the door on the other side. He threw her case into the back seat then sat down beside her. The headlights dimmed slightly as he started the engine. The car moved forward up the drive.

The last vestiges of the fog in her head wafted away. Suddenly everything was crystal clear. She remembered why she had been running down the driveway and where she had been intending to go. She had been running away from Lucia again. She had been intending to go back to Venice. She had been going to him. But he wasn't in Venice. He was there beside her in the car and he was taking her to where Lucia was.

'No, no. No, Marco,' she burst out. 'Please don't take me back to the villa. I don't want to go back there. Lucia is there and I don't want to see her. She arrived this afternoon with Liza and Ian. I saw them come so I left. Please Marco, don't take me back to the house.'

Her urgent pleading seemed to fall on deaf ears. He didn't stop the car, reverse it and go down the driveway. He went on driving slowly and carefully around the bends. The powerful beams of the headlights silvered the cypresses, then blazed into the courtyard, striking sparks of light from the shiny black limousine. Golden light spilled out from the downstairs windows of the villa and its pink stone glowed with a faint ghostliness against the dark trees of the hillside behind.

'I'm not going into the house,' said Sandra when he turned off the engine, having parked beside the limousine. 'Not while she is there. Did you know she would be here?'

'I had guessed she would be. I received a mesage from Ian last night, when I was in Genoa. He said that he and Liza would be coming over this way and that they hoped to call on Claire. I assumed Lucia would be with them.' He spoke quietly, matter-of-factly, then leaned urgently towards her. '*Cara*, you must go into the house so that we can find out about your injuries. You could have cracked a bone in your knee or your arm when you fell. And you must be suffering from shock. We'll call a doctor to examine you.'

'No, no, I'm all right. Nothing is cracked or broken, I fell very lightly. I wouldn't have fallen, only I tripped over my own feet. I don't hurt anywhere,' she insisted. Only inside, she thought miserably. Inside she was hurting because he had come back to see Lucia. He had guessed Lucia would be there so he had driven out to be with her instead of returning to Venice. 'I don't want to see a doctor,' she went on. 'I want you to drive me away from here, please. Oh, why don't you do anything I ask you to do?' she moaned.

'I thought I did something you wanted me to do yesterday by driving you here to see Claire,' he retorted exasperatedly, and she remembered with another pang of regret Claire saying that he must be getting fed up with her.

'Yes, you did,' she whispered, making an effort to show that she appreciated what he had done. 'And I'm grateful, truly I am. But I can't go back into the villa. I don't want to see her. I don't want to see any of them . . .' Her voice broke and she fished in her pocket for a handkerchief.

Without a word he started the engine again. The car swept round in a wide curve and headed for the driveway again. Glancing back at the villa Sandra noticed that the front door was open and someone had come out to stand on the steps waving. It was only a glimpse she had before the car was engulfed by the dark tunnel of the cypresses but she thought the person was Harry Edmonds.

At the end of the driveway the car turned right and began the descent to the village.

'So where do you want to go?' asked Marco briskly. He was cold and brisk like an east wind again, she thought unhappily. And she had done that to him. She had rejected his gentler warmer approach, pushed it away from her so he had withdrawn swiftly, returned to his mountain-top.

'I . . . I don't know. I just want to go somewhere quiet, where there aren't any people we know to interfere with us,' she whispered.

'Where were you going when I . . .' He broke off with a curse and added roughly, 'Do you realise I could have killed you when I drove into that driveway?'

'It was my fault. I shouldn't have been in the middle. I should have been more careful.' She was suddenly desperate to reassure him he wasn't entirely to blame.

'No,' he argued, 'it was my fault. You were right

about my driving too fast but I wanted to get there quickly, before Lucia said anything to you.' He laughed gruffly. 'I should have known better. I should have guessed you wouldn't have stayed there for long. I suppose you were on your way to Genoa airport in the hopes of booking a flight to London. Is that where you'd like to go now? To the airport to find out if you can get a seat on a plane to London tomorrow?'

'I already have a seat booked on a plane to London tomorrow,' she said dully. 'Harry Edmonds arranged it for me. Marco, why didn't you tell me Claire had married again?'

'It was for her to tell you, not me. I might have said something to you about it after the dinner party when we had time to talk. But ... you left and then I decided, what was the use of telling you anything? You wouldn't believe me.' His voice rasped harshly. 'Do you approve of what she has done?'

'I could hardly disapprove. Harry is such a nice person. And I'm glad now that Claire has nothing to do with Fontelli's.'

'So am I,' he said with a fervency that surprised her. 'She was absolutely hopeless as chairman. And now that she doesn't own any shares you can't accuse me any more of having married you because you're the daughter of the chairman.'

'I wonder why Francesco ever nominated her or left her all those shares?' mused Sandra.

He made no comment. They had reached the village. Turning to the right, he drove away from it to the coast road in the direction of Genoa.

'I hope you told Claire you were leaving,' he said abruptly when they had gone a few miles. 'I hope you haven't run away this time without saying where you are going, putting someone through hell wondering where you've gone and why.'

'I left a note for her telling her where I'd gone,' she said. And that had been another mistake, she thought ruefully. She had told Claire she had gone to Venice but now she had had to change her mind. She was going to London, because Marco expected her to go there; because he wasn't in Venice; because he had changed his mind about going there when he had realised Lucia was in Portofino tonight.

'Did you go through hell the other night and in April when I left?' she asked.

'You must have a strange notion of how I feel about you if you can't guess how I feel when you disappear without a word,' he replied coldly. 'What the hell do you think I'm made of? Rock?'

'Sometimes I do think that,' she countered shakily. 'When ... when you're in one of your mountain summit moods.'

'Mountain summit?' His voice crackled with surprise. 'What the hell are you talking about?'

'You. You're like the top of a mountain peak sometimes, way above me, remote, unapproachable.'

He was silent a few moments then he said quietly, 'I didn't know I seemed like that to you. I'm sorry.'

'I ... I'm sorry too,' she mumbled, aware that tears were pricking her eyes making everything seem blurred. 'I didn't know either that ... that you were upset when I left without telling you where I was going.' She sniffed, swallowed and forced herself to speak again. 'I think it would be best if you take me to a hotel near the airport to stay the night, if that's possible. I'm also sorry to take up so much of your time, to take you away from seeing Lucia.'

He swore virulently under his breath but made no other remark. The car went on, shafts of light piercing the darkness ahead. They passed other cars and other cars passed them. It was like yesterday afternoon. Nothing was said. There was nothing to say, thought Sandra. Her brain was numb after going over the situation between them and she was no longer capable of drawing any conclusion. Her last decision to go to him in Venice had been blasted to smithereens by his appearance in the driveway at the villa, and his assumption that she still wanted to go to London. He wanted her to go to London. If he didn't, why had he suggested he take her to the airport?

Lights, hundreds of them, spangled the darkness in front of Marco and Sandra. They seemed to hang in the air. They were the lights of Genoa shining from the tiers of buildings which climb the steep slopes of the bowl of green hills which is its setting. They reached and stopped at a junction where another road crossed the highway and curved off to the airport. It seemed to Sandra that when the traffic lights changed Marco hesitated about which direction to take.

'It's to the right. We should go to the right,' she said. But, as if he hadn't heard her, he drove straight across and on towards the town.

She didn't argue. She didn't care any more where she went or where she stayed if she couldn't be with him. He could leave her wherever he liked, on a street corner if he wished, and she could find her own way to a hotel. She was beginning to feel the effect of the fall. Her right knee was smarting as if she had grazed it and there was a dull throb on her right hip.

Down steeply sloping streets he drove. People thronged the pavements, as is usual in the evening in any Italian city or town. Lights glittered from shops. They drove round a wide *piazza*, where buses were lined up outside the entrance to a railway station, and turned right along a wide, modern busy street with Saturday evening traffic. An opening appeared in the kerb. The car slowed down, turned right again and swooped under a portico built out over the entrance to a hotel.

Marco stopped the car, turned off the engine. The door beside Sandra opened. She glanced up at the enquiring face of a uniformed commissionaire. He looked down at her and then across to Marco, his dusky face breaking into a smile. He spoke quickly in Italian. She caught the gist of what he was saying. He had recognised Marco and was surprised to see him back so soon. Then, holding out a hand, he offered to help her out of the car.

She stood waiting, conscious of how awful she must look in her bedraggled raincoat and torn stockings, wishing she had thought to tidy her hair while she had been in the car. Her case and a zipped holdall, which she recognised as Marco's, were taken out of the car and carried into the foyer by a porter. Another porter appeared. Marco gave him the car keys and the car was driven away to some underground parking area. Marco took hold of her arm and urged her towards the glass entrance doors which were swung open for them by the commissionaire.

Thickly carpeted floor and potted plants, soft lighting, comfortable chairs arranged in groups, people talking quietly—Sandra gave the entrance foyer a quick glance and stopped short.

'This looks very expensive,' she said.

'It is,' Marco replied. 'But since you won't be paying, why worry?'

He strode past her to the shining reception desk and she hurried after him.

'I . . . I just want a small room,' she hissed, hovering

at his side as he spoke to the woman behind the desk who was reacting to his smiling, polite manner, smiling back coyly until she noticed Sandra. Then her eyebrows went up in shocked surprise and her facial expression changed to one of sneering criticism, as if she couldn't associate this shabby-looking young woman, with the wild red-brown hair, with the handsome wordly man who was filling out the registration card. Sandra turned away quickly, her cheeks burning, as if she had been caught soliciting Marco's favours like a woman of the streets.

She felt his hand at her elbow, gesturing her towards an alcove where there were lifts.

'You don't have to come up to the room,' she whispered as he got into a lift with her and three other people. 'Which floor is it on?'

'The top. A penthouse suite,' he replied casually.

'But I don't want to stay in a penthouse suite!' she protested, her voice rising querulously as she turned on him.

'I do. I stayed here last night. The view from the top is magnificent.'

'But you can't stay with me—' She broke off realising that the two men and the woman who were in the lift were staring at her. Lowering her voice she said, 'What about Lucia? She'll be expecting you.'

'Shut up,' he said with such force that it was like a slap on the cheek. 'I'm tired of hearing you bleating about Lucia.'

Shock silenced her. Biting her lips to hold back tears she sank back against the wall of the lift beside him, wishing a hole would open up in the floor and swallow her up. Never had he been so rude to her. She glanced furtively at the other people in the lift. They looked embarrassed and she guessed they had understood what Marco had said. Judging by the clothes she guessed they were Americans. Much to her relief they all got out when the lift stopped at the twelfth floor.

As soon as they were gone and the lift doors were closed again she said in a tight little voice without looking at him, 'There's no need for you to be so rude in front of other people.'

'I wasn't being rude. I was being honest, straightforward and expressing my feelings. I thought that's what you like,' he retorted.

The lift stopped again. The door slid open. Once again he took hold of her arm, pushed her forward with him. They stepped out into a square hallway, hushed and scented. There were four penthouse suites, a door in each corner of the square. One door was open. The porter had apparently arrived before them with her case and Marco's holdall.

There were three rooms in the suite: a sitting-room, a bedroom with a huge double bed, and a tiled bathroom. The furniture, the curtains and the upholstery were of the best quality. Sandra, after inspecting the rooms, lingered by the wide windows of the sitting-room, which would open out on to the balcony in warm dry weather. She decided the view must be of the harbour because there was a big pool of blackness where only a few lights glittered, and beyond that a shining shimmering path, where the silvery radiance of the first-quarter moon was reflected in the sea. Behind her she could hear Marco speaking in Italian, and she wondered if he was phoning the Villa Montagna, to speak to Lucia and explain why he wasn't there, why he would be late arriving. Miserably she gazed down at the light-sprinkled darkness,

wishing . . . oh, God she didn't know what to wish for
any more!

'You can't see much now,' said Marco at her back
and touched her shoulder. 'Tomorrow you'll be
surprised.' His other hand touched her other shoulder
and she stiffened guessing he was going to kiss her
neck. She jerked away, turned to face him.

'Why do you want to stay here for the night?' she
demanded shakily.

'Can't you guess?' His lips curved tantalisingly and
his eyes glinted with icy sparks.

'No, I can't. I don't understand you. I thought you
were . . .' She stopped. She had been going to mention
Lucia again and she suddenly remembered the rebuff
he had given her in the lift. 'Why aren't you going
back to the Villa Montagna?' she whispered.

'Because I'm hungry, and I'm tired. And I'm
damned if I'm going to drive that coast road in the
dark again.' He put his hands on her shoulders again
and drew her towards him. She recognised the
darkening of his eyes, the slight parting of his lips as
he gazed at her mouth. 'I also feel like making love to a
woman, you happen to be on hand and you're my wife.
Why should I waste time driving to Portofino when
I've got all I want right here—food, bed and a
woman——'

'But . . . but . . .' Hands against his chest fending
him off she shook her head in bewilderment. 'Oh, I'm
tired too,' she blurted, drawing her breath in sobbing-
ly. He didn't want her particularly. He wanted a
woman, presumably any woman. 'And I'm beginning
to hurt where I fell,' she complained. 'I can't do what
you want. I can't. It's too much to ask of me knowing
that you were going to see . . .' Her tongue caught on
the roof of her mouth just in time stopping her from

saying Lucia and she said instead, 'Knowing that we're going to be divorced.'

His hands slid from her shoulders slowly, down her arms and fell to his sides.

'Okay,' he murmured and moved away from her. She stood for a few moments holding her breath, waiting for him to say he would leave. There was a knock at the door. He called out to whoever was knocking to enter. The door opened and a waiter came in bearing a tray with a bottle of wine and two glasses. Sandra turned away and went quickly through to the bathroom, closed the door and locked it from the inside. Sitting on the edge of he bath, she let the tears flow freely at last.

After a while, her sobs subsiding, she went over to the wash-basin to bathe her face and caught sight of herself in a mirror. What she saw made her gasp in dismay. Her face, except where it had been blotched by salt tears, was chalk-white; her eyes were puffy slits and her hair, oh God, her hair! She touched it with curious fingers. No wonder the receptionist had stared at her in a funny way. Her hair was sticking out spikily and would have been the envy of any punk-rock performer. She was really surprised Marco had tried to take her in his arms just now, that he hadn't made some cutting remark about her appearance.

She turned on the bath taps, then stripped off her clothes and examined her body. She had only one big bruise on her right hip, she had grazed her right knee and there were a few bruises on her shins. But that was all. She had escaped lightly from her fall. She was lucky to be alive; Marco could have killed her. He must have felt as shocked and shaken as she had been by the accident.

Stepping into the bath, she lay down in the scented

water and closed her eyes. If Marco knocked on the bathroom door or attempted to enter she didn't hear him, because she floated off into a doze, and came to herself with a jump of surprise when she realised the water was growing cool. Sitting up, she turned on the hot tap again and began to soap herself. Already she was beginning to feel better. The relaxation had eased her tense nerves.

The hotel had provided a sachet of shampoo, toilet water and scented soap. She used them all, and half an hour later stepped from the bath to dry herself, looking with dismay at her discarded suit and blouse. She would never wear them again, she vowed. She hated the sight of them.

To get fresh underwear and her green dress she had to return to the bedroom. As she opened her case she realised how quiet the suite of rooms was. No music came from the sitting-room. No sound of voices from the TV. Was Marco in there? Or had he gone after all? Gone to see Lu—— She bit her tongue.

The green dress was horribly creased. It was unwearable. There was nothing else for it—she would have to hang it up and hope that the creases would hang out by morning. She would have to wear her nightdress and dressing-gown.

Her smoothed, drying hair beginning to sparkle with reddish lights, the lemon-coloured, quilted dressing-gown flattering her colouring, she went hesitantly into the sitting-room, bracing herself against the shock of not finding Marco there. But he was there lounging on the settee, seemingly half-asleep.

'Are you all right?' he asked, getting to his feet. He had taken off his white sweater and ski-jacket and was wearing only a dark red shirt, with his black trousers.

'You've been so long.'

'I almost went to sleep in the bath.'

'The bruises, are they bad?' He was close to her again, looking down at her as if he were really concerned about her.

'No. Only one big one, on my right hip. I was lucky, and I'm feeling much better now, just very sleepy. I . . . I think I'll go to bed.'

'But not yet. Eat first,' he ordered. 'The food that I ordered from room service has come. It's here on this trolley. Sit down and I'll bring you something.'

'No, I'll help myself, thank you,' she said stiffly.

He shrugged and walked over to the trolley where the food was in stainless steel serving-dishes being kept warm on an electric heater. One dish contained her favourite *cannelloni*, and, her mouth watering, she helped herself to it and added some of the crisp salad to her plate. When she was seated in an armchair, Marco brought her a glass of wine, setting it on a small table beside the chair. He returned to the settee to eat. There was silence.

It should have been so different, Sandra thought sadly, this feast in this room where they were together and alone, and she couldn't help remembering other times when they had travelled together and had shared meals in hotel rooms, remembering the talk and the laughter, the kisses. But now there was nothing to talk about, it seemed, nothing to laugh about, and she had rejected his lovemaking even before he had touched her. There was nothing to share except the food.

He finished eating before she did, excused himself, said he was going to have a bath too and left the room. She had some dessert, another glass of wine, put the covers on the dishes, and considered the settee. It was only a two-seater, not really long enough for her to sleep on comfortably. And she was longing to sleep. Her eyes would hardly stay open.

Yawning, she went into the bedroom. The wide bed looked tempting. Going over to it, she turned down the covers. The sheets were smooth, the pillows plump. Hesitating no longer, giving in to the weariness that was sweeping over her, she took off her dressing-gown, climbed into the bed, covered herself, switched off the lamp and plunged into a deep, soft darkness.

She woke suddenly out of am unpleasant dream and lay quietly, collecting her wits, wondering where she was for a few seconds as she stared at a wide window through which she could see stars glittering in a blue-black sky. Remembering that she was in a hotel in Genoa, she wondered next what time it was. Reaching out, she snapped on the bedside lamp and looked at her watch. It was ten to four.

Slowly she lay back against the pillow and turned her head. Marco lay on the other side of the bed. There was about three feet between them. He was on his side facing her and while she looked at him he opened his eyes and looked at her, his eyes sparkling with reflected light between narrowed black lashes.

'What's wrong?' he murmured.

'Nothing.'

'Then why are you awake?'

'I don't know. I was dreaming, I think, and had to get out of it somehow. It wasn't very pleasant.'

'Your hip . . . the bruise on it is not hurting you?'

'No. Not really.'

'I would like to see it.' He moved closer to her and pushed himself up on one elbow. The bed-covers fell away from him revealing that he was naked at least as

far as the waist. He twitched the sheet and blanket off
her and she shrank away from him.

'No. It isn't necessary for you to see it,' she said
hastily.

'I think it is. I'm responsible for you being hurt, so I
want to see how bad it is.' A hand on her right thigh,
he began to slide her nightgown up. She couldn't
shrink back any further from him without falling off
the bed, she thought wildly. Perhaps she should fall off
the bed!

The thought came too late. He had uncovered her
hip and was looking down at the purple contusion, his
hand warm on her thigh still. He muttered something
in Italian and then bent his head swiftly and laid his
lips against the bruise. Sandra gasped, not with pain,
but with the sudden dagger-thrust of desire which
stabbed through her when his hair brushed against her
bare skin. Hearing her gasp, he raised his head
quickly, to look at her with narrowed eyes.

'It hurts?' he said sharply, but he didn't move away
from her. He didn't take his hand from her thigh
either. He let it slide upwards caressingly.

'No. No more than it should,' she whispered.

He smiled at her suddenly and her heart flipped
over. Warm from sleep, his hair tousled, his glance
soft, he was a dangerous threat to her.

'It will get better more quickly now I have kissed it,'
he murmured. 'That is what my Scottish grandmother
used to say to me when I hurt myself as a little boy. But
come closer, *cara mia*. His hand left her thigh, his arm
went round her waist and he pulled her against him.
'You will fall out of bed if you don't.'

Once trapped against his hard familiar body she
was doomed. Liking the feel of him through the thin
stuff of her nightgown, she sighed and gave up the

struggle so that when his lips, tired of plundering her throat and cheeks, found her lips she was ready for his kiss, greedy for it, her mouth opening to the thrust of his tongue.

There was tenderness in the touch of his fingers as they stroked her slowly. He handled her as if she were a delicate *objet d'art* acquired by Fontelli's for sale in one of their exclusive shops, drawing from her a response of which she hadn't known she was capable. While she was in his arms, she ceased to question and doubt his love for her, and her own love poured out of her, showing itself in the way she touched him, her caresses growing more and more demanding as the ache to be one with him swelled uncontrollably, flushing her with a hot desire to feel the throb of his passion within her. A groaning mass of sensuousness, she flung herself against him and heard him laugh softly and triumphantly as he welcomed her possessive attack on his hair, his skin, his lips, taking her with an authority that defeated any last-minute withdrawal on her part.

The exploding excitement of satisfaction was followed by a feeling of awe as she floated down from the high mountain peak of shared sexual passion, down and down, light as a feather to the heat of the bed, the scents of warm skin, the thudding of heartbeats. She wanted to tell him she hadn't known such pleasure before or experienced such a closeness with him of mind and body, but a wonderful lassitude was creeping through her, and she was content to lie collapsed against him until she fell asleep, lulled by the steady beat of his heart beneath her ear.

She was wakened a few hours later by the clangour of church bells as they rang out across the city. Without opening her eyes she stretched languorously

under the sheet, vaguely aware of a feeling of
wellbeing but unable to account immediately for that
feeling. All that mattered for the moment was, it was
Sunday morning, she was lying in a comfortable bed,
and she didn't have to get up straight away.

She turned on to her right side. The dull pain of the
bruise on her hip throbbed. Last night Marco had
kissed it and said it would get better and afterwards,
oh, afterwards, he had made love to her as never
before, as if he loved her, cared only for her, and all the
misunderstandings between them had been wiped out.
Or so it had seemd unless she had dreamed the whole
scene. She opened her eyes quickly.

Marco wasn't in bed with her. The other side of the
bed, the part where she wasn't lying, stretched
smoothly before her, the plump pillows undented,
looking as if they had never been disturbed, as if
Marco hadn't slept there. Oh, surely she hadn't
dreamed he had been with her? Surely she couldn't
have felt all she had felt in a dream? Horrified at the
thought that she might have indulged in some wild
sexual fantasy during the night, Sandra gasped and sat
up, realising at once that she was naked. Surely she
couldn't have undressed herself, taken off her own
nightdress . . .

In alarm she scrambled out of bed, pulled her
dressing-gown on and went through to the living-
room, calling Marco. Sunlight slanting through
Venetian blinds gave a rippled appearance to carpet
and furniture. The trolley with the serving dishes and
plates was still there with the empty wine bottle, but
the electric warming plate had been unplugged.

'Marco——' she turned back into the bedroom
towards the bathroom. The door was open. Towels
were strewn about, damp and creased. Her sponge bag

was open on the surround of the oval wash basin.
There was nothing belonging to Marco, nothing that
said he had been there.

With a feeling of puzzled anxiety growing within
her, Sandra turned back into the bedroom. Her own
case was there on the rack provided for luggage. In the
wardrobe her dress and suit hung where she had put
them the previous evening. No clothes belonging to
Marco were there. She swung round and looked wildly
for his zipped travelling bag. It wasn't in the room
either.

A feeling that she still might be trapped in a dream
came to her as she went over to the dressing-table to
look for any note he might have left, remembering her
own note left for Claire the previous day. But the
surface of the dressing-table was bare and hard,
shining in the sunlight. It felt *real* to her finger tips.
She wasn't dreaming it was there any more than she
was dreaming the view she could see through the slits
in the blinds, a view not of the harbour from this side,
but of the buildings of Genoa, old and new clustered
together, climbing the slopes of the amphitheatre of
hills.

Back to the sitting-room, she flitted and searched
the top of the small writing table for a note. Nothing
there either. But Marco had been there, she was sure
he had. He had brought her to this room, he had eaten
with her, drunk wine with her, slept in the same bed as
her, made love to her. Her thoughts faltered. Or had he
slept in the bed? Had he made love to her? That was
the part she couldn't be sure about.

But she was sure he wasn't there now and had
possibly left. With a groaning sigh she sank down on
the settee. She had imagined it all, then. She had
imagined that everything had come right between

them, that their rapturous reunion during the night had wiped out misunderstandings. Seduced by his gentleness, by the tenderness that had expressed itself through his fingertips and his lips she had believed he loved her and wanted her back. She had forgotten that for him, lovemaking was an art in which he was highly skilled; she had forgotten his caustic remark that last night he had felt like making love to a woman, she had been on hand and his wife into the bargain.

He had gone, left her without a word, as she had twice left him, and she could only see last night's culmination of passion as another act of revenge.

Where had he gone? To Portofino to find Lucia? Suddenly she had to find out. She snatched the receiver off the phone, jabbed at a number for the operator and stood shaking with outrage because Marco could treat her with such little respect. At last she heard a woman's voice on the phone. Signora Petuli's voice. Yes, Signor Edmonds was at home.

'Sandra.' Claire for once had lost her *savoir faire* and with it the resonance of her voice. She seemed to squeek with surprise. 'Why did you leave like that? Where are you now? In Venice?'

'No, I'm in Genoa. Claire, is Marco there?'

'No. What on earth are you doing in Genoa?'

'I stayed the night here. I ... I met Marco. He brought me here but now he's gone and I don't know where he is.'

'Well, perhaps he's gone out for a walk. Or gone to church. Does Marco go to church?'

'Oh, no, no. He's left, taken his bag. He's gone. Without a word.'

'Sounds as if he's learned something from you, darling,' Claire was drily amused. 'But why do you think he would come here?'

'Isn't . . . isn't Lucia there?'

'Good heavens, no. They left, soon after dinner, thank God. I like Ian but I must admit Liza and Lucia drive me up the wall, even though Liza is Francesco's sister. She's just far too sweet for me. But they were very sorry not to have seen you again. I had to explain to them that you'd had to leave in a hurry, to catch a plane. I didn't know what else to say.'

'Did you tell them I was going to Venice?'

'No. I didn't think it was any of their business where you'd gone.'

'They must have been surprised when Marco didn't turn up.'

'Why should they be? They said nothing about expecting to see him,' replied Claire lightly. 'Where did you meet him?'

'In the driveway. He was on his way up to the villa.' Sandra had a sudden vivid memory of the violence of that meeting, its near-disaster violence.

'Coming back to see you, I would guess,' said Claire complacently. 'I thought he might be back. That's why I wanted you to stay on over Saturday. What a good thing he arrived before you'd gone too far on the way to Venice! Is everything all right now? Have you made it up?'

'No. Everything isn't all right. He's gone, left me here, I tell you! And I don't think he was returning to the villa to see me. He knew Lucia would be there. It must have been all arranged between them before he left Venice and brought me to see you . . .'

'Oh. Do you really think so, darling?' Claire asked casually while Sandra struggled to catch her breath. 'I don't. I mean, I don't think even Lucia would make an arrangement like that now she's engaged to be married.'

'Lucia is engaged to be married?' gasped Sandra.

'Yes. To the most charming American. He was with them, with Ian, Liza and Lucia, when they came. That's why they called in, actually. To introduce him to me and to you. Brad, he's called—Brad Carter. He's with Fontelli's too, the American branch. Sandra, are you still there? Are you all right?'

'Yes. I'm still here.'

'So what are you going to do now?'

'I . . . I suppose I'll catch the plane to London,' said Sandra dispiritedly.

'Oh, dear,' sighed Claire. 'Well, phone me from London to let me know you've arrived safely,' she added, gently but firmly disengaging herself from Sandra's problems. 'It was nice seeing you. Harry has become quite fond of you already and he hopes that we'll see you out here for Christmas. Let us know what your plans are.'

'Yes, yes, I will. Goodbye.'

Sandra put down the receiver. Plans. Plans for Christmas. She didn't have any plans for anything. She didn't know where to go, what to do. Getting to her feet, she walked into the bedroom, found her handbag and searched for and found the piece of paper on which Harry had written the time of departure of the plane for London. Then she looked at her watch.

She had missed the plane.

Flinging down her handbag, she rushed into the bathroom. A quick shower and she was out again, dragging her much criticised suit off the hanger, thankful she had brought a change of blouse with her. Within fifteen minutes of having found out she had missed the plane she was descending rapidly to the foyer with her case.

Much to her relief, the woman who had been at the reception desk the night before wasn't there and she was greeted by a pleasant young man who told her in reply to her rapid-fire questions that yes, Signor Morosini had checked out and had paid for everything and yes, he had left a message to say he had gone back to Venice.

'Is there anything else I can do to help you, *signora*?' he added.

'Is there anywhere open near here where I could find out about planes to London?' she asked.

'At our travel information desk. Over there,' he replied.

'Thank you.'

At the desk he had indicated, she told the woman of her plight, how she had missed the plane to London on which she had booked and how she wondred if there was another that day. The woman did some telephoning and came back, shaking her head.

'I am sorry, *signora*. There is no space on the next flight to London from Genoa. There isn't a seat until tomorrow morning's flight. Shall I book you a seat on that?'

'No. No thank you. Just tell me where the bus station is please.'

Five minutes later she was out in the street walking in the mild sunny air in the direction of the Piazza Aquaverde.

CHAPTER EIGHT

SUNSET colours, varying from violet through rose-pink to crimson, gold and primrose-yellow stained the sky. Against this background the *campaniles*, cupolas and red-tiled roofs of Venice glowed and shimmered above the smooth, sun-gilded waters of the lagoon. Looking out from the bus that had brought her from Milan, Sandra felt the surge of excitement mixed with admiration that this view of the magical city always roused in her.

It was late on Monday afternoon, and the bus from Milan although fast had been tedious. Now she was longing to reach the Piazzale Roma, to get off the bus and embark on a *vaporetto*.

She was still feeling a little amazed at her own change of mind. It had happened on the way to Milan from Genoa on Sunday—without any conscious thought on her part, without any planning. When the bus from Genoa had driven into the airport at Milan she hadn't got off. Knowing that the bus would be going into the bus terminus of the city, she had stayed on board.

At the city terminus she had enquired the times of the buses to Venice, had found she wouldn't be able to travel on one until the next morning. She had purchased a ticket, found a nearby hotel and spent the night there. When morning had come she hadn't changed her mind but had tried to phone Marco at the apartment in Venice. He hadn't been there so she had left a message on the answering machine for him,

166

telling him the time of the arrival of the afternoon bus at the Piazzale Roma, and had said that she would be on it and would he please meet her. Later, she had phoned his office at the headquarters of Fontelli's in Mestre. He hadn't been there either so she had left another message.

She supposed she should have phoned Joan too and asked her to inform the library that she wouldn't be returning to work there. Perhaps she should have phoned Thea as well and told her not to expect her back. Why hadn't she? she wondered now. Was it because she was still unsure of Marco? Because there was still the possibility he might reject her and refuse to have her back?

The bus lurched into the wide *piazza* at last. She descended the steps, waited for her suitcase to be unloaded from the luggage compartment and looked around. Marco hadn't come to meet her so she walked across to the landing stage and went aboard a *vaporetto*.

He wasn't at the Rialto stop, either, and she felt the chilly feeling of forlornness settle upon her as she walked along the Calle Merceria. Lights were coming on in the shops. People were walking about, cheerful people, mothers with children, young lovers holding hands. Only she was alone, it seemed, on her way to see her husband to ask him if they could start their marriage all over again; begin again and try to recapture that special something they had once possessed, try to create again the beautiful fragile bubble of marital happiness.

But supposing Marco wasn't at the apartment? Supposing he hadn't received her two messages? Or supposing he had received them and had decided to be further revenged on her by not showing up? He hadn't been at the bus terminal to meet her and he could just as easily not return to the apartment tonight as a way of letting her know he had had enough of her behaviour—of her perversity, he had called it.

She walked on, her spirits dropping lower and lower. Even the spectacular sight of San Giorgio's *campanile* and dome, silhouetted against the last of the sunset flush in the sky, floating on its pool of shadow-striped, violet-coloured water, could not rouse her.

When she reached the Palazzo Fontelli she stopped to look up at the windows. No light glowed in any of them. Behind her the colours faded in the sky. A cool breeze blew off the water reminding her that while she had been in Italy, November had given way to December. It was nearly winter.

She tried the doors of the palace. They were locked. She pressed all the bells: the one for the top apartment, the one for Marco's apartment, the one for the caretaker's apartment. No one came to open the door.

She couldn't believe it. She could have sat down on her case and cried with frustration. She had come back and she couldn't get in because she didn't have a key to the front door and no one was in. Marco wasn't there.

The breeze wafted about her throat and ears and she shivered. Plunging her cold hands into her pockets, she turned and looked at the view. No colour now, only the black silhouettes of the tower and dome on San Giorgio against a grey sky in which a few stars were beginning to glint.

With a sigh she picked up her case and began to go down the steps, wondering where to stay the night, in Venice or in Mestre? She could, she supposed, go to Angela's flat again. She smiled wryly, thinking of the last time she had gone there and what Marco had believed about her and Giulio. There had been no need for Marco to be jealous, she thought now. No other man had ever wanted her but him, and now it was beginning to look as if *he* didn't want her any more. And it was her own fault. Her own silly fault.

Footsteps sounded near at hand. Reaching the bottom step, she looked round. A man was striding along, his head bowed, hands in the pockets of his sheepskin jacket. Marco. Her heart, which had seemed to have sunk to a position near her stomach, leapt up and began to beat fast and furiously.

She dropped her case, sprang off the bottom step and flung herself at him as he turned to mount the steps. He stopped short and put his arms out to catch her.

'Oh, I'm so glad you've come,' she cried, putting her arms about his neck.

'What the hell are you doing here?' he demanded. 'I thought you'd be in London by now.'

'Didn't you get my messages? I left one on the machine in the apartment for you and also with a secretary at the offices in Mestre, asking you to meet me off the Milan bus.'

'I didn't get either. I've been out all day. Brrr. It's cold standing here,' he said. 'Let's go in.'

In the lift compartment they looked at each other. Sandra felt suddenly unaccountably shy of him. She thought he was looking at her warily.

'Why aren't you in London?' he asked.

'I . . . I changed my mind,' she whispered.

'So what's new about that?' he jeered softly. 'And how long will the change last? Until the next time you suspect me of deceiving you? The next time you jump to a wrong conclusion?'

The lift stopped before she could think of a suitable retort. As she had guessed, it wasn't going to be easy convincing him that she wanted to be reconciled with him, wanted their marriage to begin all over again.

The hallway of the apartment was dark, silent and rose-scented. Marco flicked a switch and soft, diffused lighting came on.

'Are you thinking of staying the night here?' he asked politely.

'Yes. That is, if you'll let me.'

He made no comment beyond a slight shrug of his shoulders, and walked away down the passage to the master bedroom. Taking off her raincoat as she went, Sandra followed him.

'Why did you leave Genoa without waking me to tell me you were leaving?' she blurted out as soon as she entered the room.

He had put her case down and was taking off his sheepskin jacket. His suit jacket followed his sheepskin on to the nearest chair before he answered.

'I didn't see much point in hanging around,' he drawled, sliding open a door of the wardrobe. 'You were intent on returning to London, I thought. Or so you'd told me. And I wanted to be on my way early to come back here because I knew I had to see a lot of people today.' He delved into the cupboard and brought out some clothing. Tossing it on to the bed, he began to undress, taking the tie from his neck, unbuttoning his shirt. 'You were fast asleep and it seemed a shame to disturb you,' he added, slanting her a glance. 'I left a message with the clerk at the reception desk for you. Didn't you get it?'

'Yes, but not until after ...' She broke off, distracted from what she had been going to say by the sight of him without his shirt. He was wearing a white vest that clung to his muscular chest and waist. The skin of his bare arms shimmered in the lamplight as muscles bulged and rippled when he lifted a sweater from the bed and pulled it on over his head. 'You should have woken me,' she burst out. 'You should have told me you were leaving. You . . . you should have given me the chance to . . . to come here with you.'

'Should I?' His head appeared through the neck of the sweater, black hair tousled. His eyes glimmered with a mocking light. 'I did think of it, believe me. But then I changed my mind. I didn't want to seem *too* possessive by insisting that you come back here with me. I know you don't like to be regarded by *me* as one of *my* goods and chattels . . .'

'Stop it! Stop making fun of me.' she stormed and launched herself at him. She wasn't quite sure what she was going to do but she caught him off-balance, he went backwards on to the bed and she fell with him on top of him, legs sprawling against his, her breasts flattened against his chest, her face dangerously near his. She tried to push up and away from him but he prevented her by putting his arms around her and holding her against him.

'This is so sudden, *cara mia*,' he whispered mockingly and, sliding a hand up to the back of her head, he forced her face closer to his. Down and down, closer and closer until their lips met.

Warm and sweet was that kiss, a meeting of lovers who were glad to be together again and who were both trying to express through physical contact what they had so far been unable to say to each other; as it deepened Sandra felt the usual hot weakness flowing through her, the desire to let go of reality and to float through a spinning darkness with him upwards, always upwards until they surged out together into the blinding white light of fulfilment.

But the kiss came to an end. His hands hardening at her waist, he pushed her gently from him, sliding her off him until she lay backwards on the bed while he sat up and finished pulling on his sweater, thrusting his arms into the sleeves. Then he stood up and began to unzip his trousers. Turning away from her, he took off the trousers, hung them up in the closet and began to draw on a different more casual pair that she recognised as the sort he wore to go skiing.

She pushed herself up to a sitting position. It seemed to her that in spite of the way he had just kissed her he was far more interested in what he was doing and that he was thinking of something else that had nothing to do with her return to him.

'Aren't you glad I've come back?' she asked hesitantly.

In the process of buckling his belt he glanced up, a bright flash of icy light in his shadowy face.

'I'm always glad to see you, *cara*, he replied simply, slipping the tongue of the belt through a slot. 'But you must excuse me if I don't seem to be in a very loving mood, right now. I'd like to get packed up and on the road . . .'

'You're going out again? You're going away tonight?' she exclaimed.

'Yes. There is snow in the mountains. A good covering, Bernardo says. I'm meeting him up at Cortina later this evening. We should get some good skiing in during the next few days.'

Dumbfounded, Sandra sat on the edge of the bed watching as he began to stuff extra clothing into a zipped waterproof nylon holdall. She had come back to him and all he could think of was going skiing!

Gripping the silken bed-cover with her hands she bit hard on her lower lip to control her temper and at last managed to say, 'But what about your work? How can you go away and ski? Don't you have to work?'

Still squatting beside the holdall which was now bulging but not yet completely full he grinned up at her. 'I can work anywhere sweetheart. You know me. I don't have to stay behind a desk all day, in a high rise office building. There are such things as phones, message machines; I can make contact with the Fontelli executives from anywhere. And always when I'm enjoying some sort of physical activity I get my best ideas.'

She knew that was true. He belonged to the new wave of businessmen who don't need an office from which to work, who aren't tied to a desk from nine to five. But she thought he would be more pleased that she had come back

'Don't you want to know why I changed my mind?' she whispered.

He zipped up the holdall with difficulty, it was so full now, and picking it up he stood up and put it on one of the silk ottomans at the foot of the bed. Then he slipped on the red and black ski-jacket. From the end of the bed he regarded her from under slanting black eyebrows.

'Do you want to tell me why?' he parried her with another question. 'You don't have to. It is enough for me that you decided to come to Venice instead of going back to London,' he continued warily. 'I'm not even going to ask you how long you will be staying here . . .'

'I'm not going to stay here if you're going off to the mountains,' she flared, springing to her feet and whirling round to glare at him. 'I . . . I came back to

. . . to be with you, not to stay here waiting for you to come home. I . . . I thought you wanted me. The other night, in Genoa, you seemed to . . . and then you did trick me into coming back here in the first place and if . . . if it hadn't been for Lucia turning up at that dinner party I wouldn't have run away a second time. I was coming back to Venice and to you when you . . . drove into me . . .' She stopped, out of breath and stood still facing him, her breasts rising and falling.

'Then why didn't you tell me you were on your way here? Why did you let me go on thinking you were going back to London?' he demanded harshly, seemingly as angry with her as she was with him. In two strides he was before her, towering over her threateningly, his eyes blazing with icy sparks. 'Why? Why?'

'I . . . I thought you were going to the villa to see Lucia, I thought you didn't want me any more, that you were fed up with me because I . . . I'd run away a second time, because I didn't trust you. You said you knew she would be there and that's why you were going back there so I thought you'd arranged to meet her there. I didn't know until Claire told me on Sunday morning that Lucia is engaged to be married.'

'I see.' His breath hissed as he drew it in. 'So you let me continue to think you preferred a life of separated bliss, pursuing your career in London, living with some lesbian in a poky little London flat to living with me,' he said tautly.

'Thea isn't a lesbian,' she raged. 'Oh, how can you say such things?'

'Easily,' he retorted. 'As easily as you have been able to believe that I preferred to have a wife *and* a mistress. I'm just as capable of judging by appearances only, of jumping to conclusions instead of

finding out the true facts before making a decision.'
He glanced at his watch. 'Time I got going if I want to
be in Cortina before nine,' he said and grabbing up the
holdall, strode from the room.

'You'll never be there before nine,' she argued
breathlessly running after him down the passageway
to the hall. 'Only if you drive too fast.'

'So I'll drive too fast.'

'Marco, stop! Listen to me,' she pleaded, rushing
round in front of him as he strode towards the lift
doors. 'I . . . I came back because I wanted to ask you
if we could start again.'

'Start what?'

'Our marriage. I know that I made a mistake in
April believing what Lucia said about you. I know I
should have tried to trust you more and I've told you
why I didn't. It was because you're so secretive. But
during the last few days I've learned a lot about
myself.' She stepped closer to him, put a hand on his
chest and looked up appealingly. 'Please, Marco,
could we start again?'

'Only if you'll come with me now, to Cortina,' he
replied softly, dropping the holdall to the floor and
taking her in his arms. 'I know I'm possessive, and I'm
unwilling to share you with other people or with your
interest in books and libraries, but please belive me
when I tell you that I had no idea I seemed arrogant
and autocratic to you, demanding more than you can
give, expecting you to be what you're not. I love you as
you are, *cara mia*, very much, and I'll try not to expect
too much from you, if you really want to come back to
me. Will you come back to Cortina tonight?'

'I don't know where my ski equipment is,' she
muttered, her voice muffled by his jacket against

which he was pressing her as he held her tightly against him.

'So, what does it matter? We'll buy some new for you when we get to Cortina,' he said with that reckless extravagance that always delighted her even while it shocked her. He held her away from him and eyed her critically. 'It's a pity you'll have to travel there in that awful suit, but just as long as you're with me I guess I can turn a blind eye to it.'

'I'll never wear this suit again after today. Never,' she whispered fervently.

'Best to wait until tomorrow, until you have something else to wear,' he said practically.

As they walked to the Rialto they didn't talk. They didn't need to, thought Sandra happily. They were communicating without speech, messages vibrating between them. Her arm didn't feel trapped by his and she felt no desire to twist free of his domination. She was beginning to realise his seeming arrogance, his wish to buy things for her, his demand that she should go skiing with him now were, after all, expressions of his love for her. Giving her everything a woman could desire was his way of giving himself to her.

It wasn't until they were in the car and crossing the causeway that she told him of Claire's suspicions that Liza might have laid a trap for her to fall into at the dinner party at Mario's.

'Do you think that's possible?' she asked.

'Entirely possible,' he replied. 'Liza is as devious and as cunning as . . .' He broke off to laugh softly and added, 'as any other Fontelli.'

'Do you really think then that she was hoping to split us up?'

'I think she invited Lucia to that dinner as a sort of counter-move to my bringing you back to Venice. She didn't guess how you would react. She *knew*.'

'Now that makes me feel awful,' she muttered.

'Why?'

'Well, it isn't good for one's self-respect to realise other people know how you'll react to a situation. I'd no idea I was so transparent or so easily manipulated. Even you do it to me!'

'Do I?' He sounded blandly surprised but a laugh shook his voice.

'Yes, and I'm beginning to see that you not only tricked me into coming to Venice but that you've played other tricks on me since I came back.'

'Such as?' he enquired smoothly.

'Leaving me at the villa with that ultimatum and going off to Genoa and making me feel thoroughly miserable. And then leaving me on Sunday morning at the hotel in Genoa. You left without a word. I was so upset I had to phone Claire to find out if you'd gone there, if you'd gone back to the villa.'

'Now why the hell would you think I'd go there?'

'To . . . to see Lucia, of course. If only you'd woken me to tell me you were going to Venice I wouldn't have been so . . . so unhappy or worried.'

'Were you really unhappy and worried?' he asked.

'Of course I was.'

'Why?'

'Oh, because I . . . I'd thought, in the night, you still wanted me,' she whispered.

'I did want you. I still want you,' He took a hand off the steering wheel, found one of her hands and squeezed it gently. 'Never have any doubts about that.'

'Then why did you leave me?'

'You could call it a lover's revenge, if you like,' he replied. 'Now you know a little how I felt in April when you left, how I felt the other night when you left the dinner party. What did Claire say when you phoned her?'

'Oh, she thought I was silly,' she grumbled. 'But I'm glad I phoned her. She told me that Lucia is engaged to be married to an American called Brad. Did you know?'

'I knew Lucia was planning to become engaged to him. She told me at the dinner party but I didn't know they had announced their engagement. Liza doesn't like him and she had hoped that if she could show Lucia our marriage was on the verge of breaking up Lucia would change her mind about Brad in the hopes of marrying me once you and I were divorced.' He laughed again. 'What she didn't realise was that my reason for not marrying Lucia in the first place still existed.'

They had reached the end of the long bridge and were driving through the streets of Mestre, turning north on the highway to the mountains.

'What was that reason? I wish you would tell me,' she said. 'If you would only tell me some of your secrets I'd be able to understand you better. You see, I'm not used to this sort of family intrigue, with people pretending to be so charming and pleasant on the surface while all the time they are thinking how to go one better than someone else. Please tell me, Marco. I remember you said the other day you found out something that made marriage between you and her impossible.'

He was silent for such a long time she began to think that once again she had run into the blank wall of his secretiveness.

'Have you retreated to your mountain summit?' she said eventually, trying to tease him. 'Is it so hard to tell me? You know everything there is to know about me. Why shouldn't I know something about you? Are you ashamed of the reason?'

'No. But it is hard to tell you. To tell anyone. In fact I've never told anyone since I found out, partly because I was asked not to tell anyone and partly because . . .' He paused.

'Pride has stopped you?' she suggested with a sudden flash of insight into his character.

'Perhaps,' he admitted, reluctantly she thought.

'You don't have to be proud with me,' she whispered. 'I love you and I want to love you more but I can't if I don't understand. If you make it difficult for me to understand. Please tell me.'

'All right.' He sighed heavily. 'But first you must agree to keep the information to yourself and never tell anyone else.'

'I promise.'

'I've told you that Lucia and I went about together for a while,' he began slowly. 'Looking back I can see it wasn't very serious for me. I wasn't passionately in love with her or anything like that. But I enjoyed her company. She was fun to be with and we shared a lot of likes and dislikes. Being with her was more like being with a sister I'd never had than being with a lover.' He paused again and added in a lower voice, 'I suppose I should have guessed from that.'

'Guessed what?'

'That she and I are blood relations.'

'Really?' she gasped. 'How close?'

'First cousins. To my way of thinking and to the way of thinking of the person who told me, that put a taboo on us being married.'

'First cousins!' she exclaimed. 'Does Lucia know?'

'She might know by now. You see, I was so furious

with Liza after Lucia turned up at that dinner party that I told her why there wasn't a chance of me ever marrying Lucia.'

'Was she surprised?'

'Thoroughly shaken, I'm glad to say,' he replied maliciously.

She was silent, busy with this new piece of information, trying to fit it into a jigsaw of family connections. The car roared on. Scattered snowflakes whirled towards them. The lights of oncoming traffic were dazzling.

'If you and Lucia are first cousins and she isn't Ian's daughter, Liza must be your aunt,' she mused out loud.

'Right.' He sounded distant again, uncommunicative.

'Then your father must be a brother of Liza.'

'Right again.'

'An older or younger brother?'

'She had only one brother,' he said curtly. 'My father was Francesco Fontelli. Now you know, and you'll keep it to yourself if you value our marriage.'

'Does Ian know?' she gasped. Amazement was threatening to choke her.

'I'm not sure. If he does he has never mentioned the fact to me, and I didn't know until a few years ago when Francesco visited me while I was studying in the States and told me why I shouldn't even consider marrying Lucia. Liza had told him of her plans to arrange a marriage between me and Lucia, and he had decided to defeat her object. He didn't approve of the idea at all.'

'Because of the closeness of your relationship to Lucia?'

'Because of that and also because he disliked arranged marriages. His first marriage was an arranged one and he was never happy with his first wife. He believed very much in freedom of choice, and also in the freedom to love where you wish. He was still trapped in his first marriage when he met and fell in love with my mother.'

'Was that why he didn't marry her when he knew she was expecting you?' she asked.

'He never knew she was expecting his child. She never told him and I think she never knew he loved her. She left Venice soon after their brief affair, went back to Scotland and was never in touch with him again. He told me she was a very proud and independent person.'

'But if he loved her he could have got in touch with her again,' Sandra pointed out.

'He did. He wrote to her, tried to see her. She didn't answer his letters and refused to meet him.' His voice was dry. 'You will perhaps recognise her behaviour and will now understand why I tricked you into coming to Venice last week. I was beginning to see that your pride and your independent way of of behaving might come between you and me as hers came between her and my father. He didn't know about my birth until after she had died, when it was too late for him to marry her. She had told my grandparents before she died that he was my father.'

'But could he have married her? What about his first wife?'

'He had made it possible for her to divorce him so that he could be free at last to go to my mother and propose marriage, but the divorce wasn't finalised until it was too late. It was when he travelled to Scotland to see Isabel that he found out about me.'

'He must have been very surprised.'

'He was hurt more than surprised because she

hadn't told him. He told me that at first he vowed to have nothing to do with me, to leave me with my grandparents. And that was what happened until I was about nine and Ian took me with him to Venice, to tell Francesco that my grandmother had died and my grandfather was too old and infirm to care for me. It was then Francesco decided to take on his parental responsibility. He kept me with him, always saying I was the son of a distant relative of his who he was training to follow in his footsteps at Fontelli's.' Marco laughed with a touch of self-mockery. 'And I never twigged, never guessed he was my father! I always called him Uncle Frank.'

'Were you shocked when you found out you were his son?'

'I suppose I was a little, but I was more relieved than anything else. I'd often wondered who my father had been, just as you must have wondered who your father was when you found out that Claire was your mother and not Joan, and Ed wasn't your father.'

'Yes, I did,' she replied and was silent again for a while. Then she said, on a note of surprise, 'We have more in common than I'd thought. We were both born out of wedlock.'

'Both of us are love-children,' he suggested softly. 'That was the old term for persons born as we were. I think it was finding out that about you that made me more interested in you.'

'How did you find out?'

'In some ways you resemble Claire, and then after Francesco died and I was going through his papers— he made me the executor of his will—I found cancelled cheques paid to a certain Joan Clarke who lived in Surrey, England.'

'He paid money to Joan?'

'For your keep and education. He felt he owed it to Claire for asking her to give you up when she married him. Claire introduced you as Sandra Clarke and it wasn't difficult for me to put two and two together and realise you were her daughter, not her neice.'

'Claire didn't know that you knew about the cheques to Joan. I'm sure she didn't, and that she doesn't know you know now,' she exclaimed.

'She doesn't know because I didn't tell her I knew,' he replied. 'Joan has never said anything to you about the allowance Francesco made available for you?'

'No.'

'Probably because he asked her not to. He was a very secretive person.'

'Like father, like son!' she mocked.

'I admit it,' he replied equably.

'There's just one thing I don't understand, though. If he knew you were his son, his natural heir, why did he leave his shares in Fontelli's to Claire? Why didn't he leave them to you?'

'He had already made arrangements for me to inherit a handsome annuity. To have left the shares to me would have made everything too easy for me, I guess, and he was a stickler for hard work and enterprise. It might also have declared to the world that my relationship to him was closer than he had ever admitted to anyone, even to Claire. He left the shares to her, he said in a letter he left for me, because he wanted to show his appreciation of her as his wife. He knew she would be able to sell them, if she didn't want them, at a good price, and that the money she got from them would be a good income for her. He also guessed that she might want to marry again and he suggested in the letter that if the occasion should arise I should arrange for her to sell them. So I did.'

'I wish you'd told me all this before.'

'And bored you to tears?' he jeered.

'I wouldn't have been bored. Just fascinated. And it would have helped me to understand you better. Oh, Marco, why have we made everything so hard for ourselves?'

'Because we're still learning to know each other and to love each other, I guess. No one ever said that marriage or any other close relationship is a bed of roses,' he remarked drily. 'So don't think because we've decided to resume our marriage we're not going to have misunderstandings in the furture; we are. I can only hope that we've both learned from this rather violent disruption of our relationship not to let any misunderstanding split us apart.'

'I hope we have, too.'

'So are you still angry with me for tricking you into coming back?'

'No. Not any more. Are you still angry with me for letting you down and running away from the dinner party?'

'Not now I understand why you did. I've had my revenge on you. Although I realise that could have backfired on me. You could have gone off in a huff to London, like my mother went back to Scotland, and the next I'd have heard of you would have been in a lawyer's letter stating that you wanted a divorce.' He reached out a hand to her again. 'We've come a long way towards understanding each other the last few days, don't you think?'

'Yes, a very long way,' she murmured with a happy sigh, and put her hand in his trustingly.

Soon they were among the mountains. The slight snow had stopped and the sky had cleared and the snowy peaks were clearly outlined against a blue-black, starlit sky. Before they reached the town of Cortina d'Ampezzo they turned off to drive along a snowploughed road that twisted up the side of a hill and ended abruptly before a sprawling wooden building from which lights blazed. Marco parked the car beside other cars and they walked quickly in the frosty air to the entrance of the building.

A blazing log fire, bright lights, and smiling faces greeted them on their arrival. Bernardo, slim and lithe in ski-pants and sweater, came forward, his black eyes twinkling. He took hold of Sandra by the shoulders and kissed her on both cheeks.

'So you are back again,' he said. 'You are well again, and you found the Contessa well also?'

'Yes,' she nodded, smiling back at him without reserve, not at all disturbed by the knowledge that Marco had covered up for her disappearance from the dinner party and her subsequent journey to Portofino by lying to his friends. 'I got back just in time to come up here with Marco.'

'Good. I'm glad you've come.' Taking her hand, he pulled her forward to introduce her and Marco to the other people in the room and made some remark in Italian that Sandra didn't catch but made everyone else laugh and clap their hands.

'What did Bernardo say about us when he introduced us to the others?' she asked Marco later when she lay snuggled up against him in the bed in their room at the ski-hotel.

'Didn't you notice anything about them?' he asked drowsily answering her question with another question.

'I noticed that none of your friends—Bernardo, Giuseppe and that tall man with the fair crinkly hair whose name I can't remember . . .'

'Kurt. He's from Austria,' he supplied for her.

'I noticed that none of them are with the same women they were with last winter!'

'That is true. All three of them have new lovers,' he replied, sliding a hand up and down her thigh while he tantalised the corner of her mouth with his lips. 'Has it occurred to you that if you hadn't come back tonight I might have come here with another woman too?' he mocked gently. 'Admit now, *cara mia*, that is why you came rushing back to Venice today. You were afraid I might find someone to take your place if you went back to London again.'

'If you had . . . if you dared, I would never have spoken to you again,' she hissed. 'You . . . you're married to me . . .'

'Don't I know it!' he groaned but there was laughter below the groan, she could feel it shaking him. Then suddenly he was serious, fiercely so, holding her tightly against him. 'And you're married to me! Don't ever forget it,' he growled into her ear, his breath tickling it deliciously. 'No more running off into the night with handsome piano-players.'

'Oh, I wish you'd forget about that.'

'Never!'

'I didn't think you could ever be jealous of someone like Giulio.'

'I'm jealous of any man who dares to look at you the way he did, the way he kissed your hand and made eyes at you.'

'But I love you, and I would never run off with another man. I've never met anyone to compare with you . . .'

'Or as wealthy as I am!' he put in drily.

'Oh, you're not thinking, surely, I . . . I've come

back because of that?' she exclaimed. 'Oh, stop being so suspicious!'

'As long as you stop being suspicious of me, as long as you swear to trust me and love me, always,' he whispered.

'I love you and I'm always going to trust you from this time forward,' she said sincerely, secretly amazed that this man whom she had believed to be so self-confident, so arrogant, needed to be reassured. 'You're my lover, my only lover,' she added, touching his face, threading fingers in his hair.

'And you are mine. Would you like me to prove it?' he whispered, growing gentle again, stroking her arm.

'Yes, please, after you've told me what Bernardo said about us,' she said pressing her length against his hard throbbing body and sliding her hands beneath his pyjama jacket to enjoy the silken feel of his skin.

'He called us the married lovers. You see, none of the couples staying here is married except us,' he murmured.

'Do you think he was making fun of us?'

'Possibly, but only because he's jealous because I have a wife and he doesn't. I liked what he said about us because it's true, has been true all along. We are lovers and we are married. So let's celebrate those two facts, shall we, in the usual way?'

'Yes, please,' she whispered, pressing against him urgently and, putting all suspicion and distrust of him behind her, she rejoiced in being with him again, floating through the spinning darkness of sensual delight, knowing at last that it was as much an expression of his love for her as it was of her love for him.

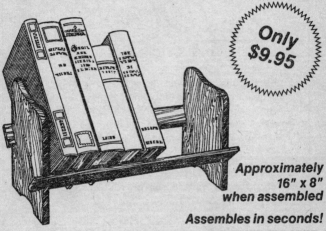

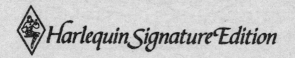

Harlequin Signature Edition

Carole Mortimer

Merlyn's Magic

She came to him from out of the storm and was drawn into his yearning arms—the tempestuous night held a magic all its own.

You've enjoyed Carole Mortimer's Harlequin Presents stories, and her previous bestseller, *Gypsy*.

Now, don't miss her latest, most exciting bestseller, *Merlyn's Magic*!

IN JULY

In August
Harlequin celebrates

The 1000ᵗʰ *Presents*

Passionate Relationship

by
Penny Jordan

Harlequin Presents,
still and always the No. 1 romance
series in the world!

Available wherever paperback books are sold.

PR1000